Fear overtook her face.

"As much as I don't want to go back there alone, I have no choice."

"You're not alone."

Conner mentally shook away the crazy thoughts. When Darci decided to let a man back into her life, it would be someone who had what it took to be a father and husband. That someone wasn't him.

Darci shook her head. "I won't put you in danger. This is my fight, not yours."

"You're wrong."

"Just who are you?"

"The missing woman is my sister. The night she disappeared she called me. Said she was scared and on her way over." He swallowed past the lump in his throat. If only...

No. Second-guessing himself was wasted energy. All the regrets in the world wouldn't change anything.

"And?"

He met Darci's eyes. "She never made it. Your boss apparently got to her first. And from the look of things, he'll get you next."

Carol J. Post writes fun and fast-paced inspirational romantic suspense and lives in sunshiny central Florida. She sings and plays the piano for her church and also enjoys sailing, hiking, camping—almost anything outdoors. Her daughters and grandkids live too far away for her liking, so she now pours all that nurturing into taking care of two fat and sassy cats and one highly spoiled dachshund.

Books by Carol J. Post

Love Inspired Suspense

Midnight Shadows
Motive for Murder
Out for Justice
Shattered Haven
Hidden Identity
Mistletoe Justice

MISTLETOE JUSTICE

CAROL J. POST

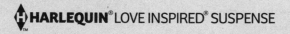
HARLEQUIN® LOVE INSPIRED® SUSPENSE

Recycling programs
for this product may
not exist in your area.

™ LOVE INSPIRED BOOKS

ISBN-13: 978-0-373-67723-8

Mistletoe Justice

Copyright © 2015 by Carol J. Post

www.Harlequin.com

Printed in U.S.A.

Enter His gates with thanksgiving and His courts with praise; give thanks to Him and praise His name.
For the Lord is good and His love endures forever;
His faithfulness continues through all generations.
–Psalms 100:4-5

As always, I want to thank my family
for your encouragement and support.
And special thanks to Mom Roberts and Mom Post
for promoting me to all your friends!

Thank you to my critique partners,
Karen, Dixie and Sabrina. You have a great eye for
seeing the things I've missed. Your input is invaluable.

Thank you to my editor, Rachel Burkot,
and my agent, Nalini Akolekar. I'm so blessed
to be working with both of you.

And thank you to my husband, Chris.
If I had it to do over again, I'd do it all over again.

ONE

Gravel crunched beneath the tires of the old Corolla. Beyond the reaches of its headlights, the darkness was thick. A full moon had begun its ascent, but hidden behind the acres of pine forest, it wasn't much help. The mine was an eerie place at night.

Darci Tucker rounded the final bend, and the view opened up. The office building stood to the left. Ahead and to the right, mounds of dirt rose in the slanted moonlight, a mini-mountain range against a dimly lit sky.

She turned into the parking lot and tightened her grip on the wheel. Two cars sat in front, a white Mercedes and a silver Lexus. The Lexus wasn't familiar. The Mercedes was. When she'd left work forty minutes earlier, the place had been deserted. Now her boss was back. Mr. Wiggins wouldn't appreciate her interrupting his after-hours meeting. But she'd left her phone on her desk and wouldn't return until Monday.

She circled around the building and stopped at an unmarked door. Maybe she could slip in through the employee break room without bothering anyone. Rupert Wiggins was the chief financial officer of P. T. Aggregates and her direct supervisor. But he had his hands in all the operations. And he was a tyrant. During her five and a half months of employment, she'd never been the recipient of his wrath, but she'd seen him ream out enough others to know she'd rather avoid that temper.

When she stepped from the car, a cool breeze swept her hair into her face. She tucked the strands behind her ear and pulled her jacket more tightly around her. In mid-November, some parts of the country were bracing for a long winter. Not Florida. Its first cold front of the year had lost its bluster before reaching the Georgia-Florida line.

She crept toward the building, key in hand, and peered through the window. The break room was dark, but dim light came from elsewhere, probably the hall that led to six of the offices, hers and Wiggins's included.

As she stepped inside, murmured words drifted to her. Wiggins and his guest. She tiptoed closer, and when she rounded the last corner, the muscles in her neck and shoulders tightened. Her boss's office door was open, his light on.

Then an angry shout stopped her in her tracks. Wiggins wasn't pleased. The other man responded, but she couldn't make out the words. He was hoarse, as if he had laryngitis.

"You want out?" Wiggins's voice was still raised. "It's a little too late for that now."

She held her breath, straining to hear the stranger's answer.

"I don't like the way you're doing things."

"Tough."

After another moment's hesitation, she spurred herself to action. She wasn't going through the weekend without a phone, especially after driving forty minutes to get back. She'd almost made it to Cedar Key before she realized it was missing.

She crept down the hall. Wiggins's office was at the end, but she wouldn't go that far. Interrupting him when he was angry might have serious consequences.

Wiggins continued, "We had a problem, and I took care of it. I did what had to be done."

"And you crossed a line that I wouldn't cross."

The derisive snort that followed came from Wiggins. "You haven't complained about the money you're raking in, so don't go getting pious on me."

Darci stepped into her office without turning on the light, her pulse pounding in her ears. That didn't sound like a disagreement over business practices. Not ethical ones, anyway. If they knew she had overheard, losing her job would be the least of her worries.

Before she could reach her phone, the screen lit up and a drumbeat sounded. She froze just inside her doorway, her heart lodged in her throat. Other instruments joined in, bringing the ringtone to full volume. The conversation at the end of the hall ceased.

The thud of footsteps kicked her body into motion. She flew around her desk and dived under it a nanosecond before bright light filled the room. Both men approached.

She swallowed hard and clenched her fists. Her hands were ice-cold, but perspiration dampened her palms. *Dear God, please don't let them look under the desk.* They were standing so close she could have reached out and touched their shoes.

Wiggins gave a dry laugh. "Chill. It's just her phone. You're way too jumpy."

"And you're not jumpy enough."

The voice penetrated her spiraling thoughts.

Beneath the raspy tone was the hint of something familiar.

"There's no reason to be nervous. No one's here but us."

Several excruciating moments passed before the men moved toward the door. Strength drained from her body, relief tempered with caution. She wasn't safe yet.

"How much does Darci know?"

At the raspy words, relief fled. Dizziness assaulted her, as if some unknown force had sucked the oxygen from the air. She *did* know the man. At least, he knew her.

"Absolutely nothing."

"And if she finds out?" The confidence in Wiggins's voice was lacking in the other man's.

"She won't."

"The other one did."

"Don't worry. I'll make sure she doesn't talk."

Dread knotted her insides. Someone flipped the light switch, casting the area into semi-darkness, and the men stepped into the hall. Her head was tucked and turned to the side, her neck bent at an awkward angle, her knees pressed into her cheek. But she didn't move. No matter how long Wiggins's meeting lasted, she would wait it out.

His office door closed with a soft thud, and

footsteps again sounded in the hall. Maybe they were done for the night. Wiggins always kept his door locked. Now she knew why.

The other man spoke from just outside her office. "How many people do you think can disappear before someone suspects something?"

Tension that had just started to ease returned tenfold. *Disappear?*

"It won't come to that." There was a coldness in the words that shot straight to her core. "I have ways of guaranteeing silence. Darci Tucker won't be a problem."

"You'd better not hurt her." A threat lay underneath the tone.

The footsteps moved away. Yes, they were leaving. Wiggins gave another derisive snort. He had condescension down to a science. "Sounds like you've still got feelings for my accounting manager."

The hallway light clicked off, casting her in darkness. The other man's response didn't reach her. Wiggins's next words barely did.

"You're so used to women falling at your feet, you can't get over the fact that one told you to take a hike."

Darci crawled out from under the desk and tiptoed to the doorway. Who was Wiggins talking to? Someone who'd hit on her at some point. But that wasn't much help. Since starting at P. T., she'd been asked out by several employees, as well as a couple of vendors and customers—the joys of being the only single female in a predominantly male work environment. But with a special-needs four-year-old who required her attention, she wasn't in the market for any of it.

She emerged from her office and crept toward the front of the building. The entry door opened then closed, and a key turned in the lock. Now alone, she slipped into the lobby, avoiding the soft light spilling in through the two large windows. Outside was Wiggins's Mercedes. The Lexus was next to it, backed in, but with the angle and heavy shadow, the license plate was obscured.

She couldn't identify the man, either. He stood at his driver's door with his back to her, the hood of his lightweight coat flipped over his head. Wiggins gave him a rough pat on the shoulder and moved toward his own vehicle. Then they both drove away into the night. A relieved breath fell from her mouth. They didn't circle around back, so she could escape unnoticed.

Anxious to be gone, she hurried toward the break room. As she stepped into the damp night air, she heaved a sigh. She could have been at her parents' house, snuggled up on the couch with Jayden while a Disney movie played on the big-screen TV.

Instead she was sneaking around in the dark like a fugitive. She could have gotten herself killed. And she still didn't have her phone. But she couldn't take it now that Wiggins had seen it.

From day one, she'd never liked him. He was overbearing, arrogant and patronizing. And crooked. Though she didn't know what it was, Rupert Wiggins was involved in something shady. Someone had found out. And at least one person had disappeared.

She slipped her key into the lock and slid the dead bolt over. *The other one did.* The other what? The other accounting manager? Wiggins had said she'd quit without notice. Maybe she'd found something and didn't want to be there when it all blew up.

Darci frowned. If she was smart, she would do the same thing.

But that wasn't an option. She needed her job. The years she ran Darci's Collectibles and Gifts had been good. But during the summer months, keeping her head above water had been difficult. So she'd sold the shop and applied for several jobs. When she landed the one at P. T. Aggregates, she'd been thrilled. First with the pay. Second with the insurance benefits. Both opened up opportunities for Jayden that she didn't have as a self-employed store owner. It had almost seemed too good to be true.

Maybe it was. Maybe her dream job would become a nightmare.

A chill that had nothing to do with the cool weather swept over her. She turned and headed toward her car. Tonight's conversation confirmed what she had suspected all along— Wiggins wasn't a man to be messed with.

Well, he had nothing to fear from her. She wasn't a sleuth. She wasn't even a detective wannabe. Whatever he was involved in, she was content to just do her job and stay blissfully ignorant.

Because if Wiggins even thought that she knew his business, he would deal with her. He had ways of guaranteeing her silence. He would make sure she didn't talk.

Maybe he would even make her disappear.

Dear God, what have I gotten myself into?

Conner Stevenson eased to a stop at the entrance to the mine and waited as two vehicles exited the gravel drive. The first was Rupert Wiggins's Mercedes. The CFO of P. T. Aggregates was well paid. That power and prestige showed in everything he did, from the way he carried himself to how he talked down to those under his command.

But Wiggins could talk to him any way he liked. Conner was right where he wanted to be. After five months of trying to land a job—any job—with P. T. Aggregates, he'd finally succeeded. The glowing recommendation from C. S. Equipment had had a lot to do with it. But nothing that Sandy, his HR person, had said was false. He really did know his stuff. He had years of experience with heavy equipment repair—overseeing, as well as hands-on. Sandy had just failed to mention that he was the owner of the company.

Conner made his way up the gravel drive, a crumpled McDonald's bag in the seat beside him. He wasn't finished working, but the trip off-site had been necessary. Not only had he been half-starved himself, but his nephew, Kyle, had needed something to eat. So had the teenage neighbor girl Conner had rooked into helping him after the previous babysitter quit. If he was lucky, she would survive until he found a replacement.

Conner sighed. He'd take it a day at a time. One minigoal had been reached—he now had his foot in the door at P. T. Today completed his first full week as their equipment mechanic.

Actually, tonight would complete it. His first week on the job, and he'd almost been whipped by a Caterpillar.

But after cleaning the carburetor, installing a new manifold and changing a couple of hydraulic cylinders, he was on the home stretch. It was a good thing. Wiggins said the backhoe had to be running by the end of the day. He just didn't say what time.

As he rounded the back of the office building on his way to the equipment area, something moved at the edge of his headlight beams. He drew his brows together. No one should be there. The mine didn't run a night shift. He turned the wheel left and angled his pickup toward the building.

White light flooded the scene. An older red Corolla sat parked in front of the back door of the break room, picnic tables to one side. A figure stood frozen in his headlight beams, eyes wide. Dark, windblown hair framed a pale face.

It was Darci Tucker, the accounting manager. The same position his sister had held. He hadn't officially met Tucker, but he'd seen her around and knew who she was. He'd made it a point to find out. Based on what a couple of his coworkers had told him, Tucker had shown up two weeks after his sister had left.

Except Claire hadn't left. She'd disappeared. Vehicle and all.

The cops investigated, talked to her friends, neighbors and coworkers. After coming up with nothing, they'd finally given up. Maybe they would have stuck it out longer if Claire hadn't had a habit of disappearing every few years since age sixteen.

But this time was different. She'd been clean for over a year and was working a steady job. And she was finally being a mother to her seven-year-old son, had even started taking him to church.

And there was that phone call, the last time they'd spoken. She'd called to say she was on her way over. Said she'd discovered something and was scared. She never made it. And he never found out what that "something" was.

He eased to a stop but didn't pull into a parking space. Checking out Claire's friends and neighbors had led nowhere, so he'd expanded his unofficial investigation to her workplace. It looked as if he was on the right track. Apparently Wiggins's after-hours meeting had included Tucker. And judging from her deer-caught-in-headlights pose, she hadn't planned on being seen.

He lowered the window and tilted his head

through the opening. "I'm Conner Stevenson, the new mechanic."

His words jarred her into motion. She swung open her driver's door.

"Pleased to meet you." She didn't introduce herself.

"I have to finish a repair on the backhoe. It's giving me fits, but I get the impression Wiggins doesn't entertain excuses."

"Wiggins can be demanding." She gave him a slight smile, but still appeared poised to bolt at any second.

"Is everything okay?"

"Everything's fine. I just came back to get something."

His eyes dipped to her hands. One held a set of keys. The other was empty. She wasn't even carrying a purse. If she had really come back to get something, it was apparently small enough to fit inside the pocket of her lightweight jacket.

"Did you find what you needed?"

She nodded, the motion stiff and jerky. "Yep. Everything's good."

That was a lie, if he'd ever heard one. He held up a hand. "Have a nice weekend. Mine starts in about an hour, if the Caterpillar back there will cooperate."

"Good luck."

She got into her car and backed from the space. When she pulled forward, she released the clutch too quickly and the car lurched. At the edge of the building, she made a sharp turn onto the drive, and its back fishtailed, slinging gravel.

Conner frowned. Darci Tucker couldn't get out of there fast enough.

He stepped on the gas and headed into the field. Someone at P. T. Aggregates probably had information about Claire's disappearance. But he had a Caterpillar to wrestle. And he needed to get it done and get home before Jenna threw in the towel, like the four sitters before her had. No matter what kind of recommendations they came with or how much experience they had, one week with Kyle had put each of his babysitters at the end of her rope.

He could relate. That was exactly where he had been since Kyle stepped over his threshold. And he couldn't blame the kid. He never knew his dad, and now his mom was missing. He was moody and bitter and angry at the world. And Conner hadn't the slightest clue how to help him.

He brought his F-150 to a stop next to the service truck that held his mechanics' tools. He hadn't signed up for this. He was supposed to be free and single and enjoying life. He was still single. But freedom had flown out the window the moment his sister disappeared. And it had seemed like three forevers since he had enjoyed his life.

He sighed and stepped from the truck. Maybe when he was finished, he would do a little snooping. He dismissed the idea as soon as it came. The incriminating stuff was likely to be inside. What he needed to do was get to know this Darci Tucker, which wouldn't be an easy task. According to his coworkers, she kept her guard up. As the only young, single woman in the company, she probably felt like a guppy in a tank full of sharks.

But he wasn't going to hit on her. And not because she wasn't attractive. She was. She was short—a good eight or nine inches less than his six feet. Her dark hair reached her shoulders, its soft, silky waves begging to be touched. With those expressive blue eyes that sparkled with life and that spontaneous smile that so often lit her face, she possessed a down-to-earth beauty that had piqued his interest from the get-go.

But he had too much on his plate to think about romance, which was a good thing. His prospects had totally dried up over the past six months. Women weren't looking for men with baggage, especially in the form of a seven-year-old with a stinkin' attitude and a smart mouth.

He opened the back doors of the service truck, pulled out a set of wrenches and approached the monster backhoe. He would figure out a way to get to Darci Tucker. Because he had no doubt—Claire didn't just take off. She finally had her life on track. She liked her job. She loved her son. And she'd found the contentment that had always eluded her. She didn't walk away from it all. At least not by choice.

If Wiggins was involved, he was good at concealing it. Tucker wasn't. She had guilt written all over her.

Or maybe that wasn't guilt. Maybe it was fear—not at him having seen her, but of something much more sinister.

The same fear his sister had felt.

Sharp white light spilled from the fluorescent fixture overhead, chasing the shadows from Darci's office. She dropped her purse and a small cooler on the floor of the closet then twisted the wand on the miniblinds. Outside, fog blanketed everything. It was a dreary Tuesday.

But the gloominess wouldn't last. In another

hour, the mist would burn off and the sun would continue its ascent, blazing a path upward in a beautiful blue sky. Florida wasn't called the Sunshine State for nothing.

She slid into the swivel chair behind her desk. She enjoyed her job. Even though she wasn't a CPA, her bachelor's degree in accounting and finance, along with her years running Darci's Collectibles and Gifts, more than qualified her to be the accounting manager at P. T. Unfortunately, none of her courses had included the chapter on dealing with difficult bosses.

She reached into her in-basket and picked up the stack of time cards piled there. Her first task of the day would be running payroll. Then she would work on the October financial statements, along with her staff meeting report, a job she had hoped to finish last Friday.

Friday. The now-familiar disquiet settled over her, and she swallowed hard. She'd come so close to getting caught. If her phone had rung on her way out, when she was sneaking down the hall...or if Wiggins had looked under her desk...

But he hadn't. Although he'd stood less than two feet away, he hadn't known she was there. *Thank You, Lord.* As long as it stayed that way, everything would be fine.

Unfortunately, the new mechanic had caught her leaving. Even stopped to introduce himself. Conner something. She remembered him, had seen him in the break room several times that week. He was the kind of guy women noticed—green eyes that sparked with restrained humor, honey-colored hair that always looked casually tousled and a bearing that radiated confidence. Yeah, hard to miss.

Hopefully, he wasn't much of a talker, because if he said anything to Wiggins about seeing her there...

As she began alphabetizing the time cards, worry gnawed at her. Her chances would be better if she hadn't acted so guilty. Maybe she should just talk to the mechanic and ask him not to tell anyone about seeing her Friday night. But that would make her look even guiltier. No, she'd better keep her mouth shut and pray the mechanic did the same.

She had just finished payroll when a familiar voice drifted down the hall. And she almost dived under her desk again. Jimmy Fuller owned a large commercial construction company and bought aggregate from P. T. He also insisted on hand delivering his checks. It gave him three or four opportunities a month to hit on her.

Footsteps drew closer and Fuller's athletic

frame filled the doorway. With that deep golden tan and sun-bleached hair, he was used to women throwing themselves at him.

"Hello, beautiful."

She laid the time cards on her desk. Let the other women have him. Those model looks were wasted on her. So were the pickup lines.

"Hello, Mr. Fuller." She stayed with the formal address. He wasn't much older than she was, maybe thirty-five to her twenty-six. But she wouldn't get too chummy with him.

He crossed his arms and leaned against the doorjamb. "Come on, Darci. When are you going to start calling me Jimmy?"

"Probably never. I'd only be encouraging bad behavior."

He threw back his head and laughed. "I'm crushed. But I'm not giving up. If I keep coming in here almost every week, I'll eventually talk you into going out with me."

"You can tell yourself that if it makes you happy."

He crossed her office and handed her a windowed envelope with a check inside. "No, what would make me happy is if you finally said yes."

He started to laugh again, but his laughter turned to coughing. When he was finished, he pulled a cough drop from his pocket. "Excuse me. I'm getting over a bad sore throat. No love ballads today." He unwrapped the lozenge and put it into his mouth. "I'm just now getting my voice back."

Realization slammed into her. Fuller had lost his voice. Just like Wiggins's visitor. She replayed phrases in her mind. The man had a slight Southern accent. So did Fuller. And Fuller had asked her out. Numerous times. Wiggins had said that she'd told him to take a hike. And she had, in so many words.

But did Fuller have feelings for her, like Wiggins claimed? Probably not. With guys like him, love had nothing to do with it. It was all about the thrill of the chase. Once they had what they wanted, the challenge was over and they were soon off on their next adventure.

But what did she know? Having not dated in five years, she was pretty rusty. Fuller was possibly the mystery man. She would try to avoid him. Of course, she'd been doing that for the past five and a half months. Easier said than done.

After Fuller left, she pushed both him and Wiggins from her mind and reached for the mouse. With her October entries made, it was time to print the financial statements. As the sheets fell into her printer tray, she opened the reports folder on her computer. The latest file was the report for September, presented at the October staff meeting.

She drew her brows together. Where was the report she'd created last week? Granted, she hadn't gotten that far. It was mostly just notes of things she needed to include. But she would rather not have to start over.

Maybe she'd saved it to her local drive instead of clicking through to the server. A few seconds later, she heaved a satisfied sigh. There it was, under *My Documents* on her *C* drive...

Right below a folder titled *D. Tucker Personal.*

What in the world? She hadn't created that folder. She had no reason to. She didn't do anything personal at work.

She clicked on the folder and two files appeared. One was labeled *Transactions.* The other was untitled. They were both created Saturday, 8:58 and 9:01 p.m. She clicked on one, then the other, frowning at the security window that popped up. Both were password protected.

The air whooshed out of her lungs and she flopped back in her chair. There was only one reason for those files to be on her computer. Someone was setting her up.

The man with the raspy voice didn't want

her hurt. But Wiggins didn't have to hurt her. All he had to do was frame her, making it impossible for her to go to the police without implicating herself.

A weight pressed on her chest, and she struggled in a breath. Burying her head in the sand was no longer an option. Neither was leaving P. T., at least until she made sure that nothing would follow her and eventually land her in jail. The problem was, she had no idea where to start.

The last one did. The words circled through her mind, as disturbing as when she'd first heard them. And her next step became clear—she needed to talk to the prior accounting manager.

She logged on to the payroll program and brought up terminated employees. Claire Blackburn was near the beginning of the list. After pulling a Post-it from the dispenser, she jotted down the address and phone number. She would try to contact her tonight.

And maybe she should check out Jimmy Fuller. She logged on to the Division of Corporations website and did a search for his company name. Nothing strange there. The business address matched what she used for billing. James Fuller was listed as the president. The vice president was…Lori Fuller? Her eyes shot back up to the president information. Same address. Not only was Jimmy Fuller a sleazy womanizer, he was married.

Without warning, Wiggins's doughy figure filled her doorway. She jumped and clicked off the site. His eyes darkened with suspicion as he stared down at her, eyebrows dipping toward the bridge of his nose, the edges of his mouth turned downward. When he crossed his arms, the gesture wasn't playful, as when Fuller had assumed the same position a short time earlier. And it wasn't done to show off rippling biceps, as she always suspected with the younger man. No, Wiggins's pose was meant to intimidate. It was working.

"Goofing off, are we?"

"No. You startled me." She held up the small stack of paper. "I just finished printing the financials."

Wiggins shook his head, his eyes scolding. "I know what you're doing. You'd best let sleeping dogs lie, or you'll get bit." Without giving her an opportunity to respond, he stalked down the hall toward his office. Except Wiggins didn't stalk. More like swaggered— the cocky gait of a man who thought too much of himself.

What was he, psychic? How did he know she was snooping?

She reached for the mouse and moved her report to the proper location. Wiggins had never been her favorite person. When she'd applied for her job, she'd interviewed with Peter Turlong, the owner, who divided his time between their Florida and Georgia mines. But since acquiring a mine in South Carolina four months ago, he'd left the Florida location in Wiggins's hands. He might live to regret that decision.

Meanwhile, everyone was forced to put up with Wiggins. He didn't just run a tight ship. He micromanaged every employee there. And she was no exception. Every report she did, he went over with a fine-tooth comb.

But when he'd stood in her doorway glaring down at her, he hadn't been concerned about her work performance. He'd been afraid she was snooping. A man with secrets had every reason to be afraid.

Wiggins was making a big mistake. She had her hands too full with her own issues to worry about the business of other people. But now that he had involved her, he'd left her with no choice.

First she would try to talk to Claire Blackburn. Then she would go to Cedar Key police officer Hunter Kingston, not in an official capacity, but as a friend.

And she would pray like crazy that she could find a way to escape the noose that was tightening around her neck.

TWO

Darci's eyes shot open, and she lay tense and alert, the remnants of a nightmare still holding her in its grasp. In her dream, she'd discovered something important, although she couldn't remember now what it was. She had looked up to see Wiggins watching her and she had run. She was still running when she awoke.

But it wasn't the nightmare that had awoken her. It was something else. Every instinct she possessed seemed to warn her of impending danger.

She waited in the darkness, but there was nothing. Just a lingering sense of unrest, as if somewhere beyond her awareness, something evil had penetrated the security of her world.

Then a soft *shhh* pierced the silence, and her senses shot to full alert. Had the sliding glass door just moved back in its track? Muffled footsteps sounded on the vinyl tile floor, confirming her fears.

She thrust the covers back and sprang from the bed, ignoring the panic showering down on her. Her son lay sleeping in the next room, twenty feet from whatever menace had just entered their haven. She snatched her phone from the nightstand and paused at the doorway to peer down the hall. A flashlight beam made wide sweeps of her living and dining area. As long as he didn't shine it down the hall… *God, please protect us.*

As she crept toward Jayden's room, her heart pounded against her ribs, and her breath came in shallow gasps. Once inside, she silently closed the door and turned the lock. A nightlight cast its dim glow through the room, over the sleeping form of her precious little boy. She needed to call 911 without alerting the intruder or awakening Jayden. Maybe from inside the closet.

Nestled between his clothes and a stack of toy-filled crates, she touched the three numbers. Moments later, a soothing voice came through the phone, and the panic she had managed to hold at bay broke through its bounds. Her words tumbled out in a harsh whisper, and she began to shake.

"Help me, please. Someone's in my house."

After verifying the address and promising that help was on the way, the dispatcher stayed on the line offering words of encouragement. They did nothing to still her pounding heart or calm her frayed nerves.

When she emerged from the closet, Jayden stirred, and she moved to the side of his bed. If he woke up, she would have to keep him quiet. He didn't talk unless prompted, but he sometimes cried. As she watched, he drew in a deep breath and let out a sigh, then returned to the rhythmic breathing of sleep.

"Are you still there?" The dispatcher's question cut across her thoughts.

"Yes." She spoke in the softest whisper.

"The police should be there any minute."

She swallowed past the lump of fear that had congealed in her throat and mentally ticked through the items in Jayden's room. If only she had something she could use to defend them.

Jayden had a bat and a baseball. Unfortunately, they were made of plastic. And he had a pistol, but it shot foam Nerf balls. Her best bet was to pray that the intruder didn't kick down the door before the police arrived.

Sirens sounded in the distance, and she sagged against the wall. A few more minutes. Actually, the intruder had likely already run out the back door.

The squeal grew louder then died. Law enforcement was out front. She released a pent-up breath. Once the officers were inside and she knew for sure the intruder was gone, she would open the bedroom door.

Jayden sat up suddenly and climbed from the bed. She circled around and caught him before he reached the door.

"Sweetheart?"

He turned toward her, his eyes wide in the dim glow of the night-light.

"Mommy's right here." She picked him up and held him against her chest. Little arms went around her neck, and she pressed a kiss to the top of his head, breathing in the berry scent of his shampoo.

In another part of the house, the sliding glass door slid back farther in its track and footsteps sounded against the vinyl floor, multiple sets this time.

The last of the tension fled. She thanked the dispatcher and ended the call. A few minutes later, a knock on Jayden's door accompanied a deep male voice.

"Levy County Sheriff's. Everything's clear. It's all right to come out."

When she emerged from the room, two deputies stood in the hall. The older one smiled down at her. "Are you all right?"

"A bit shaken up, but fine otherwise." She squeezed Jayden more tightly.

"And the little guy's okay?"

She returned the deputy's smile. "He didn't wake up until you guys got here."

He stepped back to let her pass. "We need you to look around and see if anything is missing."

She made her way toward the living room. She wouldn't bother checking her room. If the intruder had come down the hall, she would have heard him. Except for the two bedrooms, the vinyl tile ran throughout the house.

She stepped into the combined living and dining area. The deputies had turned on the lights. Envelopes lay strewn about the small dining room table. She pointed that direction.

"They went through my mail." When she'd laid it there, it had been stacked in one neat pile. But as near as she could tell, they hadn't taken any of it.

She circled the kitchen, still holding Jayden. All the cabinet doors and drawers were closed, just as she'd left them. So far, nothing appeared disturbed, other than her mail. She crossed the room to the living area. Six files sat in a stack on the coffee table. Except they weren't as neat as when she'd gone to bed. It was as if someone had checked the labels, sliding each file over a half inch to see the label beneath.

She nodded toward the stack. "I think he touched these."

"What's in them?"

"They're vendor and customer files, work I brought home with me yesterday." Hopefully, he wouldn't press her further.

Before leaving the office, she'd pulled files for four other customers and two vendors who had asked her out, just in case the mystery man was someone other than Fuller. If Claire had stumbled across Wiggins's secrets, the proof was likely contained in the paperwork at the mine. But after poring over each file and researching the companies online, she'd come up with nothing.

And her attempts to call Claire weren't any more successful. She couldn't even leave a message. After Claire's outgoing message, a computerized voice announced that the mailbox was full.

Darci sighed and met the older deputy's eyes. "I don't understand how they got in."

"Through the slider."

She had guessed that much. "But I had it locked."

"It wasn't very secure." He led her back through the dining area to the door. "I would recommend getting a Charley-Bar. Or at the least have someone drill a hole and put a pin through here." He indicated a point several inches from the top, where the frames of the two doors crossed.

"I'll do that." And the sooner the better. She'd never been nervous about staying alone. But knowing someone had come into her house while she and Jayden slept changed everything.

The deputy moved to unlock the front door. "We'll dust the slider for prints, along with your dining room table and coffee table. And we'll see what we can pick up on your mail and files while we're at it." He swung the door open and turned back around. "Any idea who might have done this?"

Her gaze traveled back to the files sitting on the coffee table. Wiggins. He wouldn't have done it himself, but he was behind it. After slipping the files into her bag, she had glanced up to see him standing in her doorway. She'd hoped he hadn't seen anything.

Apparently he had.

She opened her mouth to say so, then had second thoughts. What if Wiggins had already redirected any trails of wrongdoing to her? What if she got an investigation started and it led to her arrest?

She shook her head. "I can't think of anyone."

Guilt pricked her. But she wasn't lying. She really didn't know who had broken in to her house.

The deputy studied her. She'd hesitated too long.

"If you think of anyone, let us know."

She gave him a sharp nod.

Already it was starting. Wiggins was making sure she didn't talk. He didn't have to threaten to make her disappear.

The thought of going to jail and leaving her parents to raise her child was enough to seal her lips so tightly a crowbar couldn't pry them open.

Conner followed Kyle up the stairs at Natures Landing Condominiums, pleasantly full from dinner. All week long, he'd hoped for an opportunity to talk to Darci. There was something about her, a sweet innocence that was at odds with the idea that she could be involved in anything sinister. The more he thought about it, the more convinced he became—she was in trouble.

But both times their paths had crossed in the employee break room, Darci had brushed him off and hurried back to her office. He hadn't followed. Though he'd tried to come up with a plausible reason why the mechanic would need to meet with the accounting manager, he'd drawn a blank.

Then yesterday, a fellow employee had mentioned that Darci had a son and spent weekends at her parents' place in Cedar Key. So as soon as he'd gotten off work tonight, he'd packed two bags, loaded up Kyle and embarked on a minivacation.

Kyle reached the top of the stairs and ran full speed toward their room, excitement bubbling over. In fact, he'd been buzzing with eagerness from the moment they hit Cedar Key. Conner smiled. He would enjoy it while it lasted. All too soon, they would head back home and he'd have the old Kyle back—the sullen boy who found fault with everything anyone did for him.

But Conner couldn't blame him. Overnight, he'd been ripped from his home and friends in Crystal River and dragged to Chiefland. No wonder the kid was messed-up. And it was far from over. Next week they had Thanksgiving to get through. Four weeks after that, Christmas. By then, he'd probably be back with his grandparents. That had been the initial plan. But a week after Claire's disappearance, Conner's stepdad had had a heart attack, followed by a quadruple bypass, and his mom couldn't care for both of them.

When Conner got to the door, Kyle was still struggling with the lock, so he reached up to help him. Five seconds later, Kyle burst into their rented condo. Conner sighed. Too bad kids didn't come with troubleshooting guides, because this one needed fixing, and he didn't have the manual, tools or experience to do it. He'd never planned to be in this position. His determination to keep his relationships casual had guaranteed that he would never have to take on the role of husband or father. Until now.

With his stepdad's heart attack, Kyle's care had fallen on him—the least qualified man on the planet. His own father had been loud and abusive. The stepdads that followed hadn't been any better. Once his newest stepdad fully recovered, Conner could give Kyle back. Meanwhile, he'd be saddled with an angry, rebellious kid, and Kyle would be stuck with the world's sorriest excuse for a father.

By the time Conner closed the door, Kyle had settled himself on the nearest bed and snatched the remote from the nightstand. Bursts of sound filled the room as he advanced through the channels.

"Get your pajamas on and your teeth brushed first."

With a groan of protest, Kyle flung himself to his feet, then lifted the Avengers duffel bag onto the bed. "Then can I watch whatever I want?"

"No."

"Why not?"

"Did your mother let you watch anything you wanted?"

Kyle fished through the bag and pulled out a pair of pajamas. "No."

"Then I won't, either."

"Is that so she won't be mad at you if she comes back?"

If she comes back. "Yeah, something like that."

At first it was *when*. Now, six months later, it was *if*. At seven years old, the kid was already facing reality.

Kyle disappeared into the bathroom and came back out two minutes later, dressed in his pajamas, toothbrush and toothpaste in hand. The clothes he took off were probably on the bathroom floor, and his teeth were likely not as clean as they should be. But tonight, Conner chose to let it go.

Once Kyle had settled himself back on the bed and resumed his channel search, Conner picked up the duffel, then shook his head. The entire bag was now a wadded, twisted mess. If he left it like that till morning, the kid would go through the weekend looking as if he'd just crawled out of bed.

Conner pulled out a shirt and folded it, then removed a pair of shorts. When he reached for another item, he hesitated. He had uncovered the corner of a book.

He glanced at his nephew. Kyle wasn't a reader. He knew how to read, but he didn't do it for pleasure. And since school was out all next week, he'd told Kyle his homework could wait till later. No way was he getting a jump on it. He was a major procrastinator, unless it involved video games.

Conner pulled out the book, then drew his brows together. Kyle with a diary? It was hard enough to get him to do his assignments. He'd never keep a journal.

Which meant the book had probably belonged to Claire.

Anticipation surged through him. During that quick phone call the night she disappeared, all she'd told him was that she'd found something. She hadn't given him much to go on. Maybe the details he needed were in her diary.

He opened it to the first page. Definitely Claire's handwriting.

"No!" Kyle's scream reverberated through the room. Before Conner had a chance to prepare, Kyle leaped up and slammed into him, knocking him onto the bed. "That's Mommy's. You can't have it." He snatched the book and held it to his chest as tears welled up in his eyes.

"It's okay, buddy." Conner kept his voice low, soothing. "I was just straightening your clothes." He lifted a hand and smoothed back Kyle's hair. "I won't take it without your permission."

Kyle calmed, then swiped at his eyes, as if embarrassed to be seen crying. "You promise?"

He held up a hand. "Scout's honor. But I'll read it to you, if you'd like."

Kyle shook his head. "I don't need you to read it. I can read it myself. We're learning cursive."

Conner frowned. He wasn't surprised. The private school he'd put Kyle in had a good reputation. And his sister's handwriting was impeccable. He'd have to try another tack.

"Will you let me read it? Mommy wouldn't mind. She was my sister, you know."

He cringed at his choice of verbs. No matter

how he tried to cling to the hope that Claire would one day walk back into their lives, he still found himself thinking of her in the past tense.

Kyle didn't seem to notice. "No, it's a special book. Just me and Mommy can read it."

Without waiting for a response, Kyle climbed back into bed and slipped the diary under his pillow.

Conner sighed. If he was going to get a look at what Claire had written, it was going to have to be after Kyle went to sleep. Unfortunately, tonight Kyle would probably outlast him.

For the next hour, Conner drifted in and out while Kyle watched TV. Then he awoke with a start. He'd fallen into a heavier sleep, even started to dream. He sat up and looked over at Kyle. The bedside light was on and the TV still played, but Kyle was fast asleep.

He stood and circled around to the other side of Kyle's bed. He was sprawled out in the middle, his head between the two pillows. The scowl that usually marred his face during his waking hours was gone in sleep. He looked at peace, as if his biggest worry was whether Santa would bring him that favorite toy for Christmas. As if heartache hadn't so recently touched his young life.

When Conner started to slide his hand under

the pillow, guilt pricked him, and he pulled back. Kyle had made him promise he wouldn't take it. Well, he wasn't taking it. He was just borrowing it.

But if Kyle caught him, he would never trust him again. He would probably even hate him, at least temporarily. Conner frowned. He'd be less likely to get caught if he could slip another book under the pillow in its place. He had only one with him, a spy thriller he'd thrown in at the last minute. It was close to the same size as Claire's diary, just a little thicker. It was even a hardback.

He retrieved it from his bag, then crossed the room to again stand beside Kyle's bed. His heart pounded as he pulled Claire's diary from under the pillow and slid the thriller in in its place.

After tiptoeing around to his own bed, he arranged the pillows behind his back. Claire disappeared May 20. There was probably no reason to go back to the beginning of January. He put his thumb at the one quarter point and opened the book. His gaze fell on the left side, April 1.

Claire's perfect handwriting filled the page. She was upbeat, happy. Wiggins hadn't come in to work that day. And she had spent the evening planning Kyle's birthday parties. Two of them. Saturday would be the party with his friends at Chuck E. Cheese's. Then Sunday would be dinner with Mom and Tony and Uncle Conner. She ended the entry with "My sweet baby boy—he's the joy of my life."

Conner's heart twisted. No wonder the book was so precious to Kyle. Even though everyone believed his mother had walked away from him, the proof that she loved him was right here in black and white.

He continued to read, flipping page after page. Claire struggled with depression. That was no secret. She'd taken the brunt of the abuse from each of the men who had occupied their home, as well as the perverted affections of father number two. The latter, she'd kept buried until a few weeks before she disappeared.

But she was doing well, even though she was working for a tyrant who got some sick thrill from humiliating her. In reading her journal entries, it seemed two things were keeping her going—her love for her son and her hatred for Wiggins.

Throughout April, there was no hint of what she'd found that put her life in danger. Finally, he came to an entry that made him sit up a little straighter. May 5, two weeks before she disappeared, an irregularity showed up on the bank statement. She didn't go into detail, but it involved a large cashier's check for the supposed purchase of a piece of equipment, money she was sure ultimately went to Wiggins.

Between May 5 and May 20 were several more entries about how she was spying on Wiggins, listening outside his door, even sneaking back after closing to eavesdrop on meetings. Her last entry was on May 19. Something was going down the following night. Then she'd have everything she needed to have Wiggins put away.

That was the last entry. May 20, she never made it home.

He closed the diary and slid from the bed. Kyle suddenly turned on his side, slipping his hand under the pillow. A soft word escaped his mouth—"Mommy."

Conner froze, afraid to breathe. But Kyle didn't wake up. Several minutes passed before Conner was ready to try to switch out the two books.

Once finished, he made his way back toward his own bed with a sigh. Kyle was going to have to part with the diary. The evidence inside wasn't much, but maybe it would be enough to warrant an investigation into the accounting records of P. T. Aggregates and Rupert Wiggins personally.

After changing into some gym shorts, he slipped into bed and turned off the light. He didn't know much more than he had before. He didn't have details. And he didn't have any proof.

But one thing was certain. Something happened the night of May 20. Claire witnessed it.

And it likely got her killed.

Darci tipped back her head, letting the sunshine warm her face. Voices filled the air, shouts and squeals of happy children. Jayden's wasn't among them. She drew her gaze back to the cluster of playground equipment. Children of all sizes swarmed over its surface. Her own little guy was climbing the stairs to one of the slides, silent as always.

She sighed and turned toward Hunter Kingston, who sat next to her on the bench. For the past several minutes, he had listened without commenting as she told him everything that had transpired over the past eight days. As of last night, she had another bit of information to add. After trying for two days to get ahold of Claire Blackburn, she'd finally made the trip to the address in Crystal River and knocked on the door of apartment number twelve. It was occupied by a young couple with a baby. They had lived there four months. Claire was gone.

Talking to neighbors had provided even worse news. Claire hadn't just moved away. She'd disappeared. It was even investigated by the police. Did she leave willingly? Or had she uncovered something crooked and Wiggins— or someone—needed to shut her up?

When her gaze met Hunter's, he was frowning.

"Are you sure you don't want some Levy County detectives on this?"

"I'm positive." She didn't want to make an official report. What she needed was advice. Or maybe she just needed someone to listen, to let her know that she wasn't alone. Because frankly, she was scared.

Her eyes dropped to her hands, now folded in her lap. "I'm so afraid that if the authorities check into this, I'll be the one who gets charged. Wiggins's partner won't let him hurt me, at least for the time being. Short of killing me, the best way to guarantee my silence is to frame me. Judging from those password-protected files on my computer, I'd say he's done exactly that."

Hunter's frown deepened. "I don't like it. You need law enforcement on your side."

"If I was sure they would *be* on my side, I'd be all for it. At this point, I'm more likely to be looked on as a suspect than a victim." She crossed her arms and again sought out Jayden. He'd reached the bottom of the slide and was circling around to do it again.

"I don't know. I can't imagine someone seriously thinking you're wrapped up in anything shady. There's usually money involved. No offense, but you're not exactly living in the lap of luxury."

Maybe Hunter was right. She drove an older car and lived in a small rented house. Her bank balance was nothing to get excited about, either. But she had no idea what kind of evidence Wiggins had compiled against her.

She heaved a sigh. "I'll think about it. In the meantime, maybe you can check out Wiggins."

He pulled a small notepad from his shirt pocket. "Full name?"

"Rupert Wiggins."

"Do you have a social or at least a date of birth?"

"I can get both. They're in my payroll program. I've just got to look it up without getting caught." Worry knitted her brows, kick-starting the beginnings of a headache. "Wiggins has always watched me. That's the way he is, with everyone. But now it's different. It's as if he knows I'm onto something."

Hunter shook his head, his eyes heavy with concern. "Get me his info, and I'll find out what I can. But don't take any unnecessary chances. I really don't like it that someone came into your house."

"Trust me, I don't, either."

"I'd feel a lot better if you'd let me create a case and get an official investigation under way."

"The mine isn't in your jurisdiction."

"Cedar Key has a reciprocating agreement with Levy County. I think they'd let me be involved. I'd rather be helping you beat trumped-up charges than attending your funeral."

He had a point. But hopefully, he wouldn't have to do either. "Let me find out how big of a mess I'm in first."

Hunter tucked the notepad back into his pocket and rose from the bench. "All right. But be careful."

"I will." She forced a smile, then watched him walk away. Maybe she was crazy talking to a cop. But Hunter wasn't just a cop. He was one of her closest friends. He knew her well enough to believe that she would never be involved in anything illegal, no matter how guilty she looked. But if Wiggins planted enough evidence against her, it would be out of Hunter's hands.

She pulled her phone from her pocket and glanced at the time. Another fifteen minutes, and she would head home for lunch. By then, Jayden would be sufficiently worn-out. Not for a nap—he'd outgrown naps some time ago—but one of his videos would entertain him while she chatted with her mom.

"Mind if I join you?"

Darci started at the male voice next to her. When her eyes met familiar green ones, her stomach lurched. "Conner."

He'd traded his mechanics' coveralls for khaki cargo shorts and an olive-colored polo shirt that he filled out rather nicely. The fact that she noticed bothered her. When he grinned, the fact that he noticed that she noticed bothered her even more.

"What are you doing here?"

"We decided to take a minivacation."

We? She followed his gaze to where a blond-haired boy stood at the top of one of the slides. The boy waved, and Conner waved back.

She raised her brows. Conner didn't strike her as the fatherly type. The possibility piqued her interest, even though she didn't want it to. "Is he yours?"

He watched him come down the slide, then turned his gaze on her. "Yes and no. He's my sister's, but she's…gone." He hesitated on the last word. "So I guess you can say he's mine."

She nodded. What did he mean, *gone*? Had

she passed away or abandoned her son? He didn't offer, and she wasn't going to ask. "Have you been to Cedar Key before?"

"Several times. First time with Kyle, though."

She let out a relieved sigh, shaking the ridiculous notion that he'd somehow followed her here. He had a history with Cedar Key, like so many other people in the area. It was a favorite tourist spot, quaint, artsy and so different from the usual overbuilt, congested vacation destinations in Florida.

"Have a seat." She angled her head toward the other end of the bench. Since she had never said he could join her, he was still standing.

He sat next to her. "Thanks. How about you? Are you vacationing, or do you live here?"

"Neither. I grew up here, and my parents still live here. So Jayden and I come back and spend our weekends with them." Maybe that was more than she should have told him. But he didn't seem the stalker type. Jimmy Fuller could learn a thing or two from him.

"So which one is yours?"

She inclined her head toward the slide. Jayden was on his hands and knees in front of it, the momentum having toppled him forward.

"The one in the red shirt at the bottom of the slide."

As she watched, another boy slid down and fell on top of him.

Conner cringed. "Is he all right?"

She stood and watched as the boy rolled to the side and Jayden pushed himself to his feet. He shook his hands, then patted them together, trying to get rid of the sand. The playground was mulched, but too many feet had scattered it.

"He's all right. He's a pretty tough little boy. Doesn't cry much." *Doesn't talk much, either.*

He approached her then, palms up, and after tucking her water bottle under her arm, she brushed off his hands. Sand bothered him. A lot of things bothered him.

When she was finished, he reached for her water bottle.

She shook her head. "What do you say?"

He stretched higher, and she repeated her question, still holding the bottle out of his reach.

He dropped his arms. "Wawa, peas."

She handed him the bottle and turned to Conner. "We need to go. Mom's putting lunch on the table at one o'clock sharp."

"Then you'd better not be late. Kyle and I will be here through tomorrow. Hopefully, our paths will cross again."

The smile he gave her made her stomach

flip-flop. She was usually immune to charming men, no matter how good-looking. But seeing Conner play the father role had a completely unexpected effect on her. He had to be a pretty caring, unselfish guy to take on the responsibility of his sister's kid. There were a lot of men out there who didn't even take responsibility for their own. She knew that firsthand.

After waving farewell, she walked with Jayden to her car. Chances were good that Conner would get his wish. Cedar Key wasn't that big. Their paths likely *would* cross again.

The jury was still out on whether that would be a good or a bad thing.

THREE

Conner pulled the kayak onto the beach at the edge of the city park. The temperature was a perfect seventy-two degrees, but he had worked up a sweat. Although both of them had had paddles, most of the time Kyle's had lain across his lap. But the kid had had fun, and that was what mattered.

He started up A Street with Kyle at his side, and when he got to the corner, he glanced left down Second. A block away, a familiar red Corolla stopped at the curb. The door swung open, and Darci stepped into the street. A little farther down, a charcoal-colored Escalade also pulled to the side.

Uneasiness gnawed at the edges of his mind. When he found Darci at the park, the same vehicle had sat facing the playground, the driver still inside. At the time, he'd thought nothing of it. But twice in one day? Maybe it was a coincidence. Or maybe someone was stalking her.

Instead of crossing Second, he turned left and began making his way down the sidewalk. Darci folded her seat forward and leaned into the back. When she straightened a minute later and shut the door, Jayden stood next to her, his hand in hers.

Conner waved a greeting. "Looks like my wish was granted. I *did* get to see you again."

She returned his smile with a dazzling one of her own. Too many times in the past few days, he'd caught her with her mouth drawn into a straight line, creases of concern between her brows. Now, in the relaxed atmosphere of Cedar Key, that smile was back. And he liked what he saw. With those big blue eyes, cute, upturned nose and cheeks rosy from her time spent in the sun, she projected a warmth and wholesomeness that drew him in.

He came to a stop next to her. "What are you up to?"

"I'm paying my friend Meagan a visit." She lifted a finger and pointed to a store across the street. A watercolor painting stood displayed in the front window. The sign above the door read Darci's Collectibles and Gifts.

"Is that you?"

"I'm the Darci in Darci's Collectibles and Gifts, but the store isn't mine anymore. I sold it to Meagan."

"To go to work for P. T.?"

"Yep."

A shadow seemed to pass across her features with the single word. Worry settled in her eyes and her jaw tightened. She was probably regretting that decision.

She turned toward the store. "If you want, I'll introduce you."

He followed her, casting another glance down the street. The Escalade was still there, its driver obscured behind the tinted windshield. He squinted into the sinking sun. Even without the tint, he wouldn't be able to identify anyone at that distance.

As soon as he stepped inside, his gaze circled the store. A half-dozen paintings stood on easels near the front, each signed M. Kingston. Necklaces and earrings hung on two rotating display racks, and rows of shelves held a variety of vases, statues and other knick-knacks. Most of it looked fragile.

He reached for Kyle's hand. "There are too many breakable things."

As expected, Kyle tried to pull free. "I won't touch anything."

"I know you won't." Conner tightened his hold.

Kyle gave in with a heavy sigh and a hard drop of his shoulders. There were still arguments, but the battles were getting shorter. The kid was learning that no meant no and some things weren't up for discussion. For Conner, being hard-nosed wasn't a natural character trait. But if he ever let Kyle get the upper hand, he'd never get it back.

A female voice reached him from the rear of the store. Probably Darci's friend Meagan conversing with a customer. Soon she appeared between two of the display rows. After a quick smile Darci's direction, her eyes fell on him. "Can I help you find anything?"

Conner shook his head. "I'm with Darci."

"Oh?" Meagan's gaze swept him up and down, and her eyes lit with interest.

Darci hurried to explain, "This is Conner Stevenson. He works at P. T. He and his nephew came to Cedar Key for the weekend."

Meagan's face fell, but only for a moment. Apparently she was hoping for some romance in Darci's life. Based on what one of his coworkers had told him, Meagan was setting herself up for disappointment. Jerry said Darci didn't date. Her son came first, and she shunned anything that would pull her attention away from him.

Meagan extended a hand. "Meagan Kingston, owner of this store and friend of its namesake."

Conner accepted the handshake. "Pleased to meet you."

Darci picked up a trifold piece of glossy paper from the counter and laid back both sides. "You made up a new brochure for the store."

"I did. I've got them all over around town. I think it's helping. I've been staying pretty busy."

"So no regrets?"

"Nope. It's a good venue for selling my paintings, and when things are slow, I do some sketching."

While Darci and Meagan talked, Conner's eyes dipped to the two boys. They were both being good, but Kyle was starting to get antsy. He took a step closer to Jayden.

"What's your name?"

Jayden didn't respond. He was turned, his eyes fixed on one of Meagan's paintings displayed near the door.

Kyle patted Darci's hip. Before Conner could scold him for his bad manners, Darci stopped midsentence to focus solely on Kyle.

"Why won't he answer me?"

"You have to get his attention. But he doesn't really talk."

Kyle was silent for a moment, as if he was digesting her explanation. "Are you his mom?"

"I am."

"Where's his dad?"

Conner cringed. "Kyle! That's none of your business." So much for good manners. Darci probably thought Kyle was being raised by Neanderthals.

Darci's eyes met his, and she burst into laughter. Conner couldn't help but smile. Even her laugh was pleasant, a deep, easy, natural sound of pure enjoyment.

"You haven't been around many kids, have you? One of the first things you'll learn is that they say what pops into their heads."

Conner relaxed. Maybe Kyle's lack of manners was age appropriate. Or Darci was just being nice.

She bent over to bring her face closer to Kyle's. "Jayden's father left before Jayden was born."

"So Jayden doesn't have a father." Kyle touched Jayden's arm. "I don't have a father, either."

Jayden didn't answer, but his eyes shifted to Kyle's. Conner wasn't any expert, but Jayden seemed different from most boys his age.

A family of tourists walked into the store a few minutes later, and he and Darci bid Meagan farewell. When Conner stepped outside, he sought out the SUV. It was still there, parked in the same spot.

He looked down at Darci. "Who drives the gray Escalade?"

"What gray Escalade?"

"The one that's sitting down there." He tilted his head.

She followed his gaze then shrugged. "A tourist, I suppose. I've never seen it before. Why?"

"He seems to be taking quite an interest in you."

"Me?" She laughed, but tension underscored the sound. "Just because he's parked down there doesn't mean he's paying any attention to me."

"No, but he was at the park, too."

Her eyes widened. "Are you sure?"

"Positive. I wouldn't have noticed, except that he left right after you did. And when you stopped at Darci's, he pulled over at the same time."

The blood drained from her face, and she swayed slightly. He put a hand out to steady her. "Are you okay?"

Instead of answering his question, she drew in a deep breath and straightened her spine. He could almost see her shoring up her defenses.

"Walk with me. Please?"

"Sure."

As soon as they began moving that direction, an engine started, and the Escalade pulled from the space. It turned down D Street before they could get close enough to read the tag, then sped out of sight, headed off Cedar Key.

Darci slowed to a stop and turned wide blue eyes on him. Fear swam in their depths. He lifted an arm to drape across her shoulders and pull her close, then caught himself. From everything he'd heard about her, that would be a sure way to send her running.

He lightly touched her arm instead. "Who is he?"

She shook her head. Maybe she really didn't know. But she knew more than she was telling him.

She spun and began walking back toward her car. But he wasn't going to let her go so easily. In order to help her, he needed answers.

"Darci, tell me what's going on."

She opened the door and lifted Jayden into his car seat. Once she had fastened him in, she straightened. "I don't know."

"You're afraid. I can see that." And it was tearing him up.

She put a surprising amount of force behind her words. "If someone's stalking me, I think I have reason to be afraid."

"I agree. Any idea who it might be?"

She hesitated, her eyes searching his. Was she trying to decide whether she could trust him? Was he sure he could trust her with his own secrets?

Finally she shook her head. "I don't know."

She slid into the driver's seat, but before she could close the door, he stepped into the opening.

"When I saw you leave the mine last Friday night, you were wound up tighter than a spring. What were you doing there? Had you just met with Wiggins?"

"No."

"Then what were you doing?"

"I already told you, I went back for something." Some of the fear had retreated from her eyes, and her tone now held annoyance.

"What?"

"My phone. I'd charged it earlier in the day. I got almost to Cedar Key when I realized I'd left it."

He continued to study her. Something wasn't adding up. "If that's all you were doing there, why have you been trying to avoid me?"

She depressed the clutch and started the car. "I've been busy."

"I don't buy it, Darci. You've been more than

busy. You've been scared. Tell me what you're afraid of. I want to help."

She stared at him, indecision set in her features. When she finally spoke, steeliness had crept into her tone. "Look, I don't know what's going on. But whatever it is, it's not your concern. I appreciate your offer to help, but I'm not your responsibility."

"No, you're not. But I recognize fear when I see it. And as a guy, I can't stand idly by."

She reached for the door handle. "Let it go, Conner. You don't have a stake in this."

"Don't bet on it." He stepped away, sliding his hand along the top of the door until it rested on the corner. She wouldn't confide in him, and he wasn't ready to blow his cover. But he could get her headed in the right direction. "Check the April bank statement."

Then he stepped back and shut the door.

"What?" The closed window muffled her voice.

He circled around the car to where Kyle stood under a tree, breaking twigs off low-hanging branches and throwing them. When he reached the other side of the Corolla, Darci had rolled down the passenger window.

"What am I looking for?"

"The purchase of a piece of equipment.

Cashier's check. But don't let anyone know what you're doing."

He took Kyle's hand and started down the sidewalk. Her words trailed after him.

"Wait. Who are you?"

He didn't stop, and he didn't turn around. When he spoke, the soft tone wouldn't have carried more than a few feet. But he meant every word.

"Someone seeking justice."

Darci shifted on the wooden bench and folded the sheet of paper in front of her. It was the fourth Monday of the month, and the entire workforce of P. T. Aggregates was gathered for its regularly scheduled staff meeting. A dozen employees were seated at the two picnic tables near the break room, with the others nearby.

While Wiggins talked, Darci scanned the faces of those around her. P. T. had some good employees. Many of them had been there for years. There was an air of camaraderie among them, the sense that they were happy to be there, in spite of Wiggins.

Her gaze moved to Conner. He stood with his weight shifted to one leg and a thumb hooked into his pocket. The casual pose brought to mind a men's cologne ad, even though he wasn't dressed the part. He was probably the only man alive who could project magnetism dressed in a pair of greasy coveralls.

His eyes locked with hers, and his mouth curved up in a teasing grin. Heat crept into her cheeks. But Conner was probably used to being stared at. That dazzling smile had no doubt melted more than one female heart.

Her first impression had labeled him a charmer, maybe even a playboy. Used to having his own way. But beneath that smooth demeanor was an underlying seriousness, a thread of concern that ran just below the surface. Kyle's sudden entrance into his life had likely knocked his world off its axis.

Wiggins dismissed the group, and she pushed herself to her feet. Another meeting over. Except this time, there was consolation for putting up with an hour of Wiggins—it was a three-day workweek. The mine would be closed Thursday and Friday for Thanksgiving. And, as always, she was going to spend her time off at her parents' place. The forty-five minute drive from Cedar Key was too much on a daily basis, but on weekends and holidays, nothing would keep her from her friends, her family, her church and her girls' Sunday school class.

After stepping inside, she made her way back to her office. It was almost lunchtime.

But she wouldn't be joining the other employees in the break room. She would be holed up with a sandwich and chips, putting that thirty minutes to good use. Conner had said to look at the April bank statement, but the morning had been too busy. And Wiggins had done too much hovering.

For the next hour, though, she would be safe. Her overbearing boss always spent his lunchtime behind closed doors and didn't let anything short of a nuclear strike interrupt him.

Once inside her office, Darci walked to the closet to check her phone. With her mom watching Jayden, she tried to be always reachable. A number showed up on her call log, but it wasn't her mom's. She checked her voice mail and had no messages.

She looked at the number again. It was local, a 352 area code, but it wasn't familiar. As she studied the screen, her brow furrowed in confusion. Her call to voice mail was on top, the mystery call underneath. Both had a red, right-facing arrow, indicating an outgoing call.

But that was impossible. She hadn't made any calls. She checked the time. Nine fifty. She was at the copier then. Wiggins had said he needed copies of the October financial reports before the meeting. She'd given them to him last week, but he'd apparently misplaced them.

Or maybe he hadn't. Maybe he needed to get her away from her desk long enough to make a call from her phone. Her stomach drew into a knot. With all the company phones, there was only one reason to use hers—to make it appear that she was the one who had made the call. But why?

She slid the phone back into her purse then retrieved her cooler and carried it to her desk. After taking her sandwich out of the wrapper, she set to work tracking down Conner's lead. Thirty minutes later, a file lay open on her desk, a bill of sale inside. The April bank statement lay beside it, and her monitor displayed an equipment depreciation schedule.

She pursed her lips. What had Conner been talking about? There was an equipment purchase, just as he said. The backup was right in front of her—a bill of sale on a used 2006 Case 550H LT bulldozer. But nothing was out of order.

It had apparently been purchased from an individual, a Stanley Thomas, rather than a company. That was a little unusual, but not unheard-of. Both Thomas and Wiggins had signed the bill of sale. There was even a copy of the cashier's check stapled to it.

The dozer had been added to the equipment list as well as the depreciation schedule. And it was insured. If there was anything shady about the deal, someone had taken a lot of care to dot their *i*'s and cross their *t*'s. The question would be whether said bulldozer was actually in use at the mine.

She jotted the description and serial number on a Post-it, along with Thomas's name and phone number. Conner was the one who had sent her on this wild-goose chase. He could take the time to check out what she had. And he could call the guy with a mechanical question without raising suspicion.

What was Conner doing at P. T., anyway? And how did he know about the bulldozer purchase? It happened over six months ago. And that probably wasn't all he knew. When she told him that he didn't have a stake in whatever was going on, he in so many words told her he did. He was as much of a mystery man as the guy with the raspy voice.

She refiled the bank statement and the equipment folder, then returned to her desk to bring up her email. The most recent one was from Wiggins. There was no subject. She clicked on it, then scanned the single line. I'm watching everything you do. Let it go, or you'll get hurt.

Dread trickled over her. Had he installed a camera? Her space was pretty bare-bones.

One wall held a row of file cabinets. Two held paintings, and a window occupied a good portion of the back wall, a wide closet next to it. A live dieffenbachia sat in one corner. It was good sized, maybe three feet tall. Was it large enough to hide a camera? Apparently so. How else would Wiggins be watching her?

She rose from her desk, then sank back into her chair. First she would forward the email to her personal address. She would keep proof of everything, no matter how unimportant it seemed.

And this was important. Wiggins had threatened her. In writing. The guy with the raspy voice didn't want her hurt. But she couldn't count on it. Eventually, Wiggins's patience was going to run out.

She clicked the right-facing arrow. But instead of opening a new compose window, the email disappeared.

What? She clicked on Deleted Mail. There it was, right on top. Before she could reopen to forward it, a check appeared in the box to the left, and the cursor jumped to Delete. A nanosecond later, it was gone.

She pushed herself away from her desk and put a hand to her mouth, still staring at the screen. No wonder Wiggins knew she had been looking for something. He'd been logged in to her computer. Everything she'd done, he'd observed from the privacy of his office. And he was threatening to hurt her if she didn't stop.

But she couldn't stop. Wiggins had seen to that the moment he put those locked files on her computer. She would just have to be more careful. There were things she could do, away from his watchful eyes, such as checking out the mysterious call that showed up on her phone. It was one more piece of information to give to Hunter, along with Wiggins's social security number and date of birth that she'd looked up that morning.

And then there was Conner. He was more than just a mechanic. This afternoon, she would demand some answers.

When she walked to her car at the end of the day, several employees were driving in from the mine, Conner among them. She raised a hand, and he pulled into a parking space and exited his truck.

"I have something for you." She held up the neon green Post-it, then snatched it back when he reached for it. "First, tell me who you are."

He gave her a cheeky grin. "You know who I am. You write my paychecks."

"I know your name and that you work for P. T. as a mechanic. But mechanics don't have access to the company's bank statements." She crossed her arms. "How did you know about that equipment purchase? What are you, undercover FBI or something?"

Laughter spilled from his mouth. "Nothing as interesting as that."

"So who are you?"

He released a long, slow breath. "We're both looking for answers. What do you say we work together?"

She studied him. He apparently had information she needed. Or he was connected to someone who did. How else could he have known about the bulldozer purchase? She hesitated a moment longer. Could she trust him? Something told her she could.

She finally gave him a quick nod. "Okay. Where do you want to meet?"

"You can come to my place."

She raised her brows. "I don't *think* so."

"Hey, I've got Kyle, remember? And if I don't get right home, I'm afraid I'm going to lose yet another babysitter." He rested a hand on top of her car. "Bring Jayden, and I'll even feed you. Pizza or Chinese. I don't know which. I promised Kyle if he didn't torture the new babysitter, I'd have pizza delivered. Otherwise it's Moo Goo Gai Pan." He grinned. "I'm not above bribery."

She laughed. "You do know how to keep a kid in line. I'd go for either, but I'm guessing Kyle would choose the pizza."

"Hands down. So what do you say?"

"I'll pick up Jayden and head that way. He's at home. My mom watches him at my place, gets him to his therapy appointments and everything."

Longing flickered in his eyes, maybe even regret. "You're lucky you have her."

"I know. She's awesome. I'm an only child, so Jayden is their only grandchild. The sun rises and sets on him." She pulled a notepad and pen from her purse. "Where do you live?"

"East of Chiefland." He took the items from her and jotted down the address. "I'll give you my cell number, too, just in case."

Darci nodded. "I'll meet you there in forty-five minutes."

His eyes dipped to her hand. "Are you going to make me wait for whatever's on that Post-it?"

"I guess not."

He took the small sheet and scanned what she'd written. "The 2006 Case. I just finished doing maintenance on it."

"I checked all the supporting documentation. I won't bore you with the details, but it's all there."

Conner seemed to deflate in front of her. That was apparently not the answer he'd hoped for. He shrugged. "I guess I won't know for sure until I verify the serial number."

She opened her car door and slid into the driver's seat. "I'll see you shortly." She grinned up at him. "Pizza or Moo Goo Gai Pan." If Kyle had misbehaved, Jayden wouldn't be thrilled, either.

Darci backed from her parking space while Conner made his way toward his truck. As she covered the distance between the mine and the house she rented in Gulf Hammock, a sense of weightlessness swept over her. She was no longer handling this alone. That in itself brought a wonderful sense of relief. Besides, Conner apparently had access to information she didn't have.

She glanced at the speedometer, then backed off the gas. She didn't need a speeding ticket, no matter how anxious she was to find out what Conner knew. Or how excited she was to see him, because if she was being totally honest, she would have to admit that at least part of her eagerness was due to the thought of spending the evening with P. T.'s good-looking mechanic.

She mentally chided herself. She had her hands too full with Jayden to even think about sharing any part of her life with a man. The only things she and Conner would be sharing were resources. Once they each had what they were looking for, they would go their separate ways.

When she reached Gulf Hammock, she pressed the brake and made a right off of 19-98. A minute or so later, she flipped on her signal and slowed for a final turn. A vehicle some distance back slowed, too. Uneasiness slid through her. It was a dark SUV.

She completed her turn, then made frequent glances in her rearview mirror. The SUV didn't turn behind her. But that wasn't much consolation, because during the moment it passed through the space reflected in her rearview mirror, she was able to identify it—a gray Escalade. The uneasiness turned to dread, congealing into a cold lump in her gut. She may as well have led the driver to her house. With no garage, her car would be parked right out front. She should have been more careful. Instead, she'd been thinking about Conner, completely oblivious.

Finger by finger, she loosened her grip on the wheel. Maybe it wasn't the same SUV. There were probably lots of people in Levy County who owned gray Escalades. Even if it was the same one, all the driver seemed to be doing was watching her. If he had wanted to hurt her, he would have made his move by now.

She turned into the driveway and stopped next to her mom's Intrepid. The mental pep talk had done nothing to soothe the anxiety churning inside her. No matter how she looked at it, someone was stalking her.

When she stepped inside the house, her mom sat in the recliner with Jayden squeezed in next to her, *The Velveteen Rabbit* propped across their laps.

Her mom's eyes met hers. "Hi, sweetheart. How was your day?"

She hesitated. Other than being threatened by her boss, finding out he was spying on her and being followed home? She shrugged and went with her pat answer. "It was good." No need to worry her mother.

Jayden's eyes finally lifted from the book. Shifting gears was always difficult for him, as if he was stuck and it was hard to pull himself loose. She crossed the room to scoop him up and spin him around. When she blew a raspberry against his cheek, he giggled.

By the time her mom left and she and Jayden headed to her car, the final remnants of dusk were giving way to night. She plugged Conner's address into her GPS and backed from the driveway. Before she had gone very far, she began to doubt her decision to make the drive. The stretch of road between Gulf Hammock and Chiefland was lined with miles of nothing, lonely and dark.

As she approached State Road 24, she pushed her Big Daddy Weave CD into the player. That was where she always turned left to go to Cedar Key. Tonight she would go straight. According to the GPS, she would be at Conner's in twelve minutes.

As always, traffic was sparse. Strains of "Overwhelmed" filled the car, making her feel less alone, and she sang along. Headlights approached from behind, gradually gaining on her. As they grew closer, her hands tightened on the wheel. Any moment the driver should signal to go around her. Highway 19-98 was a four-lane road. There was no reason for someone to tailgate her when he could easily move into the left lane. But the vehicle continued to close the gap, until the headlights were a single car length from her back bumper.

Panic spiraled through her. What was he doing? Was he going to ram her?

She eased off the gas and let her speed gradually drop from fifty-five to fifty, then forty-five. Her purse was in the passenger's seat, her phone inside. Could she safely pull it from its pouch and dial 911?

Without taking her eyes from the road, she reached across the car and snagged her purse strap to pull it closer. Her eyes dipped to the speedometer. Forty.

Ahead in the distance, a set of lights moved toward her. Hope flickered. The driver probably wouldn't pay attention to two vehicles across the grassy median. But if she signaled that something was wrong by flashing her lights, maybe whoever was in the car would turn around or at least call for help.

She slid her phone from the pouch and held it against the steering wheel. The car behind her suddenly shot into the left lane and crept up beside her, then matched her speed. She dropped her phone into her lap and clutched the wheel with both hands. What was he doing?

She glanced left. It was too dark to see the driver. Or even the make and model of the vehicle. But it wasn't the SUV. It looked like an older car.

Then the space between them narrowed. He was moving over on her, trying to force her off the road. Frantic prayers circled through her mind. She jammed on the brakes and gripped the wheel so tightly that her hands hurt.

The other driver slowed also, then lunged right. Darci screamed as the crash of metal on metal reverberated through the car. Her right wheels dropped off the shoulder, and her car made an erratic path away from the highway, bouncing over a shallow ditch before coming to rest six feet from a tall pine.

Her heart pounded, and she pressed a shaking hand to her chest. The other car was gone. It had sped away while she was wrestling hers to a stop. Jayden was crying, working up to a full, terrified wail. Her phone had flown to parts unknown, and Big Daddy Weave had been silenced.

Darci opened her door, and light flooded the car. When she got out and turned, the vehicle she'd seen coming toward her was circling back. Red and blue lights flashed on top. Relief surged through her. *Thank You, Lord.* Help was on the way.

She flipped the seat forward and released the latch on Jayden's car seat. While she worked to free him from the restraints, he leaned hard against them, arms outstretched, wailing even louder. He wasn't hurt, just shaken up. It could have been so much worse. If the ditch had been deeper, she might have rolled the car.

The man with the raspy voice had told Wiggins he didn't want her hurt.

Apparently, someone wasn't listening.

FOUR

Conner turned onto 92nd Place, trying to tamp down the excitement that had been building at the thought of spending the evening with Darci. It wasn't a date. It wasn't even a cozy dinner with a friend. It was strictly business. She was coming because she was in trouble.

He glanced at the grocery bags in the seat beside him. Whether pizza or Chinese, they would need drinks. But the coconut-cream pie in the one bag was a special treat since Darci and her son would be joining them.

When he pulled into his driveway, a yellow Volkswagen Bug sat to the left. That was a good sign. His new babysitter had survived her first day of Kyle. With school out for the week, that "day" wasn't just a couple hours after school. It was one long, agonizing nine-hour period. Maybe he had finally found the perfect sitter. Either that, or Kyle had her hogtied somewhere inside.

He touched the button clipped to his visor and waited for the garage door to rise. If anyone could handle Kyle, it would be Mrs. Peggart. She'd recently retired after almost forty years of teaching.

When he slipped into the kitchen, the zing of lasers and the boom of explosions came from the living room. Kyle was playing with the Xbox. Likely the same thing he'd been doing all day. Conner frowned. Come Friday, he would have to make him buckle down and get his homework done.

Sure enough, when he walked into the living room, Kyle sat on the couch with a controller in his hands. What Conner didn't expect to see was Mrs. Peggart sitting next to him, holding the other controller.

She spoke without taking her eyes off the TV screen. "His homework's on the dining room table."

"It's finished?"

"Of course it's finished. You don't think I'd let him play without having his homework done, do you?"

"No, I guess not." He shook his head. He was still trying to digest the fact that there was a sixty-five-year-old woman sitting on his couch playing video games with his nephew. "Was he good?"

"*Good* is a relative term. What's he usually like?"

"You're the sixth babysitter in less than six months."

"Then I'd say he was a model child."

She suddenly gave Kyle a hard shove sideways. "You just blew me up."

Kyle responded with a couple of fist pumps, and she rose from the couch. After retrieving her purse from the top of the bookcase, she moved toward the front door. "I'll be here tomorrow before you leave for work."

"Thank you." Conner stifled a sigh of relief. Maybe this one was going to work out.

He locked the door behind her and stepped back into the living room. "So what do you think of Mrs. Peggart?"

"She's mean."

"Good."

He strolled into the kitchen to check the refrigerator magnet for Pizza Hut's number, then after making the call, headed down the hall to shower. He'd just reached his room when his phone rang.

The number wasn't familiar. But the voice was. It was Darci who greeted him. But something was off. Her words held an uncharacteristic tremor.

"Everything okay?"

"I've been...delayed." She took a deep breath. "Someone ran me off the road."

Fire pumped through his veins. "Where are you?"

"On Highway 19-98, about six or eight minutes away from you."

"I'll be right there."

"No, stay put. The car is drivable, and Jayden and I are fine. The cop is here, writing everything up, and they've got a BOLO out on the other vehicle."

"Are you sure you don't want me to come?" Staying home when she was out there didn't sit right with him.

"I'm positive. I'll be heading your way in ten minutes. Fifteen tops."

He reluctantly agreed and ended the call. By the time the doorbell rang, he was in clean clothes and had a salad made. As soon as he let them in, Jayden went for the controller that Mrs. Peggart had relinquished.

Darci stopped in the foyer, and he looked her up and down. She was still wearing the black dress pants and multicolored blouse she'd worn to work. There wasn't a mark on her. Her hair and makeup even still looked good. "You're sure you're all right?"

"I'm fine. I have a lot to be thankful for."

He raised his brows. With all the emotions circling through him, gratitude wasn't among them.

She continued, "Jayden and I are both fine. I could have flipped the car or slammed into a tree, but didn't. There was a Levy County Sheriff's deputy who saw the other vehicle tailgating me and turned around to investigate. My car is even drivable." The smile she flashed him lit her eyes. "We can always find something to be thankful for if we look hard enough."

He returned her smile, trying to ignore the effect hers had on him. It drew him to her in a way that went beyond mere physical attraction. "You must be an optimist."

Her smile broadened. "Yep. Looking for the good in situations makes everything seem much less bleak. But I can't lie. Sometimes I have to work at it."

He turned and led her toward the kitchen. "Any idea who ran you off the road?"

She shook her head. "I didn't recognize the car. It wasn't the SUV. But it wasn't random, either. After riding on my tail for a couple of minutes, he pulled up beside me, jerked the wheel right and slammed into me."

"You said someone ran you off the road. You

didn't tell me you were hit." His chest tightened. "I don't suppose you got a tag number."

"I was too busy trying to keep from rolling the car. By the time I got safely stopped, he was gone."

The doorbell rang a second time, signaling the arrival of dinner. It took some cajoling and a few threats to get both boys seated at the table. The only thing Kyle liked better than pizza was the Xbox. Conner sank into his chair. He should probably do something about the kid's obsession with video games. But he wasn't ready to tackle that issue yet.

"Kyle, would you like to say grace?"

That was something Claire had taught him, something Kyle insisted on before every meal. A month before Claire disappeared, she'd started taking him to church. And though Conner had never attended a service in his life, he found a local church and continued the habit. He couldn't say that it was helping Kyle, but it sure couldn't hurt him.

Kyle began in his little child's voice, "God is great…"

Conner started when a soft hand slid into his, and he opened one eye. Darci's head was bowed, her left hand stretched across the table to grip Jayden's, her other holding his own.

When Jayden reached for Kyle's hand, Kyle faltered for only a moment.

And Conner's heart skipped a beat.

They made a perfect picture—he and Darci and the two boys, seated around the table. Like a family.

Not that he'd had a whole lot of experience with family mealtime. When he was Jayden's age, his dad would hit the bars right after work and often not get home until after he was in bed. His mom had her own issues and usually disappeared to her room with a TV tray. That left him and Claire to battle out what show they were going to watch while they ate. Being five years older and quite a bit bigger, Claire always won.

Throughout dinner, Kyle was much more talkative than usual. He seemed to have taken a liking to Darci. Of course, over the past six months, his life had been lacking in female attention. Not that there was anything Conner could do about it. The women he dated weren't the motherly type.

When Kyle finished eating, he slid from his chair and made a dash for the living room. Jayden started to follow, but Darci reached across the table and clasped his wrist.

"What do you say?"

Several seconds passed. Finally he answered, "Scoos, peas."

Darci released him, and he, too, disappeared.

"What did he say?"

"That was Jaydese for *May I be excused, please?* I try to force him to communicate verbally whenever I can."

Conner smiled. Darci had it so much harder than he did, but seemed to take it all in stride. Suddenly his own load didn't seem so heavy.

After tossing their trash into the empty pizza box and closing the lid, he leaned back in his chair. "The kids are occupied and we're both pleasantly full..."

"So it's time to get down to business," she finished for him. Her mouth was curved upward in a half smile. She almost looked relieved.

"When I saw you leaving the mine that night, you looked as if you'd seen a ghost."

She frowned. "It wasn't what I saw. It was what I heard."

"Wiggins?"

"Yeah, and somebody else."

"Any idea who?"

"No. Maybe. The guy had laryngitis, but his voice was familiar. And he knew me, mentioned me by name."

He frowned. That wasn't good. "What did they say?"

"They were arguing. The other guy said he didn't like how Wiggins was doing things, that he'd crossed a line. Then he asked if I knew anything. Wiggins assured him that I didn't, but that if I found out, he would make sure I didn't talk."

His heart began to pound. What was the line Wiggins had crossed? Killing someone because she uncovered some kind of fraud?

"You need to be extra careful." She could be in the same position as Claire, caught up in something that was way over her head.

"I know. I would have been perfectly content to forget what I heard and go about my business. But last Tuesday, I found a folder on my computer titled *D. Tucker Personal*. Inside are two files that are password protected. The folder and both files were created the day after that conversation." She pulled her lower lip between her teeth and met his gaze. "I'm pretty sure I'm being framed."

"Have you tried getting into the files?"

She shook her head. "Wiggins is watching me, not just popping into my office several times a day, but shadowing me on my computer. He sent me a threatening email, then deleted it as I watched."

The pizza he'd eaten congealed into a doughy lump. "I'm sorry. I should never have asked you to check that equipment purchase. I didn't know you were being watched. You need to get out of there. Turn in your notice and apply somewhere else." The anxiety circling through him came out in his tone. There had to be another job she could get. He would even make a spot for her at C. S. Equipment.

"I can't. As much as I need my job, it's not just that. I can't walk away not knowing what's in those files. What Wiggins is trying to pin on me could follow me wherever I go. I can't take that chance."

"Then we need to get the police involved."

"Are you nuts? If Wiggins has been thorough, I'll be arrested." She sighed. "I talked to my friend Hunter Kingston. He's a Cedar Key police officer, and I've asked for his help in an unofficial capacity. He's going to pull up a background check on Wiggins. I'm also going to have him check out a phone number."

"A phone number?"

"Yeah. When I got back to my office after the meeting today, a call had been made from my phone."

"Why use your phone when there are phones all over the office?"

"That was my question. I haven't had a

chance yet, but I'm going to call the number and see if I recognize whoever answers. I'll see what Hunter can track down, too."

Conner nodded. "What about the files? We need to crack those passwords."

"That's impossible. The number of combinations is infinite."

"Not necessarily. Wiggins wants those files to appear that they were created by you. He would protect them with passwords that you would be likely to use."

"Like what?"

"Name, date of birth, address, et cetera."

A spark of hope flashed in her eyes, then sputtered out. "I'd never be able to try them. Wiggins is watching me too closely."

"Not on the weekend."

She put her fingers around her tea glass and began moving it in a slow circle, spreading the condensation in an oval shape on the glass tabletop. "As much as I don't want to go back there alone, I may not have a choice."

"You won't be going alone."

Her eyes shifted to his face, and something flashed across her features—tenderness, maybe even longing. She was probably used to handling everything, alone. And it was likely getting old. What would it be like to be the one to provide that companionship, to help create that undivided front?

He mentally shook himself. Now he was entertaining crazy thoughts. When Darci decided to let a man back into her life, it would be someone firm and stable, with a good foundation. Someone who had what it took to step into the role of father and husband. That someone wasn't him.

Darci's mask of independence snapped back into place, and she shook her head. "I refuse to put you in danger. This is my fight, not yours."

"You're wrong."

One side of her mouth lifted in the slightest hint of a smile. "I thought I might be. So spill it. Who are you? How did you know about the bulldozer purchase?"

"Claire's diary."

She stared at him in disbelief. "All the investigating the police did and came up with nothing, but you were able to get your hands on her diary?"

"I just found it last weekend. Kyle had it. Claire was my sister."

Her eyes widened for the second time. "You really *do* have a stake in this. What other information did Claire give?"

"Her May 19 entry said something big was going down the night of May 20. Then she was going to have all the proof she needed to have Wiggins put away for good."

"So what happened?"

"She called me. Said she was scared and was on her way over."

He picked up his glass and took a couple swigs of tea, swallowing past the sudden lump in his throat. He should have asked her where she was. If he had gone to her instead of waiting for her to come to him...

No. Second-guessing himself now was wasted energy. All the regrets in the world wouldn't bring her back.

"And?"

He again met her eyes. "She never made it. Wiggins apparently got to her first."

Darci cleared the lunch dishes off her mother's oak table and carried them to the sink. Jayden had already asked to be excused, after a couple of prompts, and had headed for the living room. She glanced at the clock. Conner would pick her up shortly. But what she really needed was a nap.

She'd thought she would sleep better at her parents' place. Instead, another nightmare had come. In this one, a car was pursuing her, the same one that had run her off the road. But she was on foot. The engine revved, and the vehicle bore down on her. When she turned a final time, instead of the car, it was the gray Escalade. She'd never been prone to nightmares, but this was the second one in a week and a half.

She closed the dishwasher door and straightened as her mom finished wiping the table.

"Sweetheart, can you check the mail before you head out?"

"Sure." Conner wouldn't be there for another twenty minutes.

All she'd told her mom was that she was going for a ride with a guy from work. She hadn't broken it to her yet that Conner would be picking her up on his motorcycle. Like all moms, hers tended to worry, sometimes needlessly. Darci used to find it annoying. Not so much anymore. Becoming a mother herself had changed her perspective.

When she passed through the living room, Jayden was seated on the couch, her mother's iPad in his lap. The sight always made her nervous, even though her mom insisted he couldn't hurt it.

She swung open the front door and stepped onto the porch. As she lifted her gaze to the road, a vehicle turned into her parents' driveway. Everything within her screamed for her to run, while at the same time held her rooted to the spot.

The gray Escalade eased to a stop fifteen feet from where she stood.

It was too late to slip back inside. The driver had already seen her. Besides, she wouldn't lead Wiggins's goon to her mom and Jayden. She would face him outside alone.

She held her position on the porch, her spine ramrod straight. Dappled sunlight shone through the tree that shaded the drive, its speckled glare on the windshield camouflaging the figure inside. The door swung open, and one foot, then the other, stepped down to the concrete.

When the driver straightened, her jaw went slack and a tangle of emotions circled through her. Wiggins hadn't sent anyone. But beneath the relief, everything inside her tightened into a knot, and a watery weakness settled in her limbs.

After almost five years with no contact, Jayden's father had decided to make an appearance.

She squared her shoulders and lifted her chin. "What are you doing here?"

A change of heart wasn't likely. Doug's number-one priority was Doug, and he didn't let anything interfere with his freedom and happiness. What he'd seen as a minor inconvenience easily remedied with his stepdad's money, she'd seen as a little life, and when Doug had given her an ultimatum, she'd walked away.

So why was he standing in her parents' driveway almost five years later?

He closed the door and sauntered toward her. "Is that any way to greet the father of your child?"

A slow, easy smile climbed up his face. That smile, full of warmth and charm, had toppled many defenses and given him access to more than one female heart. Now she recognized it for what it was—just another con job, a way to manipulate others into doing what he wanted.

She crossed her arms and watched him approach. He hadn't changed much since their college days. He had the same dark hair and even darker eycs that seemed to always hold a mischievous sparkle. But the lines of his face had matured, maybe even hardened a little, as if the world had slapped him with reality a time or two and life was no longer all fun and games.

He stopped in front of her and hooked a thumb through his belt hoop, shifting his weight to one foot. "I've missed you, Darci. You've been on my mind a lot lately."

Had she? What about during her pregnancy and the first four years of Jayden's life? Apparently neither of them were on his mind then.

She stood unmoving, arms still crossed, waiting for him to continue.

"I was crazy to ever let you go. I'd like to be a part of your life, be a father to the boy."

"It's a little late for that, don't you think?" Her tone was as uninviting as her posture.

He shifted his weight to the other foot, that ever-present confidence slipping. "I made a mistake, and I'd like to rectify it. With some of us, it takes a little longer to grow up." He flashed her a sheepish smile. This one looked more sincere than the prior one had.

Sincere or not, the last thing she needed right now was Doug's reappearance in her life. "I don't think it's a good idea. Jayden doesn't do well with change."

"Having both parents is good for a child."

When she didn't immediately respond, he lowered his voice and continued, "He's my son, Darci, and I have a right to see him. I think any judge would agree with me on that."

Judge? She swallowed hard. Doug didn't intend to take her to court, did he?

But what he said was true. He *did* have the right to see Jayden. But it would be on her terms, in her presence.

"I'll bring him out."

When she stepped inside, her mom was just

coming out of the kitchen. Her gaze dipped to Darci's empty hands. "No mail?"

"I didn't make it that far. Doug is here."

Her eyes widened and her mouth formed a silent O. But Darci didn't take the time to explain. She scooped Jayden from the couch, propped him on her hip and headed back out. She would explain later.

Her parents knew Doug. She'd dated him her entire senior year of college, and he'd spent every holiday with her family. He was an only child, raised by a meek, submissive mother and an overbearing tyrant of a man whom he hated. She'd never met his mother and stepfather. She'd had no desire to.

She stepped onto the porch and pulled the door shut. Doug took a step closer, but didn't make any move to take Jayden. Instead, he lifted a hand and gave him two awkward pats on the back. "Hey, little man. How's it going?"

Jayden turned away and buried his face in the side of her neck.

Doug dropped his hand. "I guess he's shy."

"Yeah, you could say that."

Doug searched her face. "I'd like to take you two out for dinner tonight."

"I'm sorry. I have plans." If Conner asked, she would have dinner with him. If not, she would spend the evening with her parents. If neither of those options panned out, there was always plan C—pizza and a Disney video with Jayden.

"Tomorrow?"

She shook her head.

"When can I see you again?"

"Me? Or Jayden?" Something told her he was using Jayden as an excuse to see her. "I'll allow you to visit Jayden, but I'm not going out with you."

His jaw tightened. Doug wasn't used to being told no. But he recovered quickly. "Then when can I see Jayden again?"

She hesitated. Doug wasn't creepy. But since she'd rather not see him at all, here in Cedar Key was better than alone at her house. "I'm here every weekend."

"And in Gulf Hammock during the week." One side of his mouth cocked up in a cunning smile. It was in his tone, too. He was letting her know that he'd followed her and now knew where she lived.

Uneasiness trickled over her. Doug didn't seem like stalker material. With his smooth manner and good looks, he could have his pick of attractive women. He wasn't one to waste time on a challenge. But she really didn't know him. A lot could happen in five years.

Without another look at Jayden, he bid her

farewell and got into the SUV. When she stepped back into the house, mail in hand, her mom was sitting in the recliner crocheting, vertical creases of concern pressed between her brows. Darci pushed the door shut as worried blue eyes met her own.

"What did Doug want?"

She handed her the envelopes she'd retrieved. "He claims that he wants to see Jayden, but he's decided to try to renew a relationship with me."

Her brows lifted. "And?"

"I told him no way."

A relieved sigh spilled from her mother's mouth. During the time she'd dated Doug, her parents had made known their concerns, more than once. All the flaws she'd been blind to, her mother had spotted—his irresponsibility, his selfishness, his tendency to live for today.

When she returned home single and with a baby on the way, the fact that she'd wandered so far from her Christian upbringing had broken her parents' hearts. But they had welcomed her back with open arms. So had her church. And never once had anyone said *I told you so*.

Jayden straightened his legs, the cue that he wanted down. As soon as his feet touched the floor, he ran across the room, climbed onto the couch and picked up the iPad. Darci rolled her shoulders, trying to dispel the tension that had settled there.

The situation with Doug probably wouldn't last long. As soon as he accepted the fact that they were over for good, he would once again disappear. Regardless of what he'd said, he wasn't there for Jayden. Even less so once he understood the extent of Jayden's issues. Doug didn't handle inconveniences well.

The roar of a motorcycle cut into her thoughts. It grew louder, then lowered in pitch and fell silent. Her pulse picked up. Conner had arrived.

As she hurried to the door, a shadow passed over her, extinguishing her temporary lift in spirits. Conner's presence was a vivid reminder that she had more serious issues on her plate than getting rid of an unwanted ex.

Issues like a threatening email, mysterious files on her computer, a suspicious boss watching her every move—and a predecessor who had vanished without a trace.

FIVE

Darci released her hold from Conner's waist and stepped off the bike. Although P. T.'s parking lot was empty, he'd hidden it several yards into the woods.

He swung his leg over the back of the bike and stood. After hanging both of their helmets from the handlebars, he looked down at her, his expression somber. "Are you ready to get this done?"

"As ready as I'll ever be."

She fell into step beside him and made her way toward the building that housed the offices. Dead leaves and dried twigs crunched beneath their feet, and a breeze whispered through the trees. Uneasiness tightened her shoulders. The sooner they could get done and away from there, the better she would feel.

At the break room door, she pulled a key from her jeans pocket. She hadn't brought her purse. Everything she needed was on her person. Her jacket held her phone and wallet, and a folded sheet of paper waited in the back pocket of her jeans. It contained a whole page of password combinations. Hopefully, one of them would work.

When she reached her office, Conner stayed in the hall.

"I'm going to stand guard out here, in case we get company."

She nodded. No one was likely to show up on a Saturday afternoon, but having Conner keeping vigil took the edge off her nervousness.

She pulled the paper from her back pocket and slid into the swivel chair. When she pressed a button on her monitor, the screen lit up and a second later, a seaside scene filled the space. It was her own photo, the view from her parents' back deck. Waves rolled ashore as two dolphins played in the distance. Farther out was the familiar patch of green—Atsena Otie. The custom desktop gave her something to calm and warm her during the hectic workday. Today, though, its soothing effect was lost on her.

She went right to work, opening the *D. Tucker Personal* folder, and started with the untitled file. Each of the first several dozen tries resulted in the same error message. When a page appeared, excitement shot through her.

"I'm in." The password was ridiculously easy—Tucker0417, her last name, followed by her birth month and birthday.

Conner poked his head in the door. "What is it?"

She squinted and studied the screen. "CEBBBZBZ, followed by a long number. The other two lines are similar."

"What do you think it means?"

"No idea." She shook her head. "It can't be an acronym, not with four *B*s and two *Z*s."

"Copy and paste it into an internet search."

She raised her brows. Nothing was likely to come up, but she did as he suggested. Moments later, she gasped. Dread descended on her with the force of an avalanche. A whole page of results had displayed, each saying essentially the same thing. *CEBBBZBZ* was the SWIFT code for the Central Bank of Belize.

Conner stepped into her office and, within seconds, had rounded her desk and stood with a protective hand on her shoulder. She shook her head and squeezed her eyes shut, trying to hold back the panic that was building inside her.

Conner leaned toward the monitor. "What's a SWIFT code?"

"It's like a routing number for a bank outside the US."

"And I bet what follows is an account number." His voice was low and ominous. What he didn't say was that the account was likely in her name. But he was probably thinking it. She certainly was. Hunter's argument that her financial status would eliminate her as a suspect had just gotten blown to smithereens.

"Check the next one."

She plugged in the series of letters that began the second line. "Scotiabank, Tortola, British Virgin Islands." After a few more clicks, she sank back in her chair. "Banco Central de la Republica Dominicana, Santo Domingo, Dominican Republic." She went back to the Word document and clicked Print, then sat back in her chair with a sigh.

"And in case things aren't already bad enough, Jayden's father showed up this morning. Now of all times, he's decided that he wants to be a part of our lives."

A tic started in Conner's jaw. "What did you tell him?"

"He has a right to see Jayden. Anything beyond that, I told him to forget it."

His features relaxed and something that looked like relief flashed across his face. Or maybe she imagined it. Since he had no romantic interest in her, he wouldn't care who she did or didn't date.

She pulled the page out of the printer. "I'll call the banks on Monday and check out the account numbers."

She knew what she would learn. Wiggins was making it look as if she was well paid for her part in their crooked dealings. She was caught in his web, and he was spinning the silk threads more and more tightly around her.

There was still one more file, the one labeled *Transactions*. What else had he done? Before Conner could even take up his position in the hall, she was in. This one was protected by the same password as the other one. Wiggins hadn't gotten very creative.

Of course, he intended to make it easy. If the authorities started closing in, it had to be a password that he, or they, could crack.

She leaned toward the monitor. This file was exactly what it purported to be—transactions. Although what kind, she had no idea. The left column contained dates, three pages worth. The numbers in the second column appeared to be quantities. The last column was dollar amounts.

She clicked Print and waited. First, she would compare the transactions with the Fuller Construction invoices. Then she would work her way through the other customers. If she could find a match, it might lead her to Wiggins's accomplice.

Conner returned to his post in the hall. "Did you learn anything about that phone number yet?"

"Hunter called this morning. It's to a throwaway phone, so it could belong to anybody. I've dialed it several times. Usually it goes to a computerized voice message. A couple of times, though, someone has picked up and not said anything, just held the phone and listened. And twice, someone has called me and done the same thing. I can't shake the feeling that it's all connected."

The first page fell into the tray, and the printer grabbed a second sheet. If she had to do extensive printing, she would ask to be upgraded from her old ink-jet to a laser printer.

She continued, "Hunter has also gotten the results of Wiggins's background check. Nothing except a ten-year-old fraud charge. And they were never able to track down the car that ran me off the road. We're batting zero all the way around."

"I've been about as successful as you. I finally got ahold of someone at the number you gave me for Stanley Thomas. The guy has never owned a Case bulldozer, and his name isn't Stanley Thomas. He's had the same number for the past five years, so it was bogus at the time that bill of sale was created."

The second page finished printing, and Conner's eyes widened. "Someone's coming in the front door."

Her heart leaped into her throat. Her printer was still chugging away, the last page just under halfway done. If she cut the power, the half-printed sheet would be trapped inside. And trying to cancel the job this far in would accomplish nothing.

Conner stood in the doorway with his weight shifted to his toes, as if ready to bolt. "Come on, we need to hide."

She closed the file and turned her monitor off, then sat with her arm extended, ready to grab the last sheet as soon as the machine released it. "I need to get this first." Her voice was a harsh whisper. "I can't take a chance on someone seeing it."

The front door slammed shut and muffled voices reached her. She sprang to her feet, her heart pounding against her ribs. The printer dumped its last sheet, then fell silent. As she snatched the page and put it with the others, her gaze locked with Conner's. His eyes held a wildness she'd never seen before, a wildness that was likely reflected in her own.

The voices grew louder. Two men were headed their direction—Wiggins and someone else.

She gave Conner a sharp wave and opened one of the double doors at the back. "Quick, in the closet."

It wasn't large. Floor-to-ceiling shelves occupied two thirds of the width, leaving a two-by-two-foot area on one side. But it was the best she could do. Conner stepped backward into the tiny space, and she backed in against him, because there was no other choice. She pulled the door shut with the slightest thud as dual footsteps sounded in the hall.

"How long do you think this will take?" Judging from the volume of Wiggins's voice, he wasn't more than a few yards away.

"Not long. Thirty minutes tops. And another ten or fifteen for me to show you how to use it."

Darci tensed. They were really close now, probably headed to Wiggins's office. Or maybe even her own.

A fluorescent glow appeared at the bottom of the closet door, confirming her latter suspicion. Someone had just turned on her office light.

Wiggins continued, "I need to see everything she does when I'm not here. I have some suspicions about her, reasons to believe she might be embezzling money."

Anger surged through her, along with an irrational need to defend herself. She'd never even taken a pen or pack of Post-it notes that didn't belong to her.

"Trust me." Confidence filled the man's tone. "This will capture everything she does."

Her chair creaked as someone's bulk settled into it, and her anger instantly morphed into fear. Wiggins was likely standing less than four feet away. A watery weakness settled in her legs, and she began to tremble. *Lord, please don't let them open the closet door.*

Conner's arms slid around her waist and tightened protectively around her. She closed her eyes and leaned into him, drawing from his strength. His embrace was firm and warm, chasing away the chill that had been her constant companion for the past two weeks. The gesture was intended to comfort and bolster her. Nothing more. But that didn't keep her from longing for what she couldn't have.

"And she won't know?"

Wiggins's words jerked her thoughts back to what was happening on the other side of the door.

"Not unless she really goes looking."

What was Wiggins doing? Installing cameras?

"If she *does* find it, will she be able to shut it off?"

It. One camera, apparently.

"Not likely. Disabling one of these is no problem for guys like me. But your average user doesn't have that level of technological knowledge."

"Don't count on it. Tucker's a lot smarter than what I gave her credit for."

"Quit your worrying and let me get this program installed."

Program. Wiggins was having something installed on her computer, probably a keylogger. Now he could find out everything she did while he was gone.

But that wasn't all. It would also make a permanent record of any evidence Wiggins planted against her, something for him to give to the authorities to prove her guilt and his own innocence.

She crossed her arms in front of her, putting her hands over Conner's. He believed in her. So did Hunter. But that wouldn't do her much good when everything blew up.

Because the evidence against her was mounting.

And this keylogger program was just one more nail in her coffin.

* * *

Conner bounced over the bumpy dirt drive, the cloud of dust trailing him visible in his rearview mirror. He'd finished the service on the Komatsu bulldozer and gotten everything buttoned up in the nick of time. It was two minutes past five.

Since last week's repairs, the 2006 Case was working like a charm. Its paperwork seemed to be in tiptop shape also. The serial number matched, right down to the last digit. In spite of Claire's concerns, neither he nor Darci had been able to find anything amiss with the purchase.

As he approached the office building, his gaze swept the employee parking area to its rear. Darci had sent him a text at lunchtime. It was short and sweet—We need to talk. All afternoon, he'd gone about his job with an underlying anticipation. She had apparently discovered something.

Conner pulled into an empty space and waited. Two people walked out of the building, then Darci appeared. The moment she saw him, a smile spread across her face and her eyes lit up. Warmth flowed through him. The memory of hiding in the closet and how good she'd felt in his arms was too fresh in his mind.

He stepped out of his truck. "Hey, you."

"Hey, yourself." She lowered her voice, even though her two coworkers had already gotten into their vehicles. "I came out to my car at lunchtime and called the three banks. The accounts are all in my name, $40,000 in one and almost $30,000 in each of the other two." She frowned. "Finding out I had almost $100,000 sitting in the bank would be a dream come true if it wasn't likely to send me to jail. But on a more positive note, I found a match on the transactions."

"Fuller?" He halfway hoped so. Something bothered him about the way the creep was always hitting on her.

"No, Marion Concrete Services in Ocala."

"Who's the owner?"

"I don't know. I do the invoices and they mail the checks. I've never even had to call them for anything."

She shrugged into the sweater she had hanging over her arm. The air was still, but it held a cool dampness. This time of year, there was a distinct difference in temperature once the sun dropped behind the trees.

She pressed the key fob, and the locks on the rented Ford Fiesta clicked. "I figured I'd look it up on the Division of Corporations website tonight." She patted the oversize purse she carried. "I've got their file in here, in case I need to refer to it."

"How about if we do it at my place?"

"I have a better suggestion. How about if you pick up Kyle and come to my place? The last time I drove to Chiefland, someone was out to get me."

"Good point." Although he wouldn't have let her make the drive alone anyway. For all visits in the future, he would be her taxi service.

She gave him her address, then opened the driver's door. "Don't worry about dinner. I've got it covered. Does Kyle like spaghetti?"

"What kid doesn't?"

Spaghetti, pizza, fried chicken and hamburgers. Those were Kyle's favorites. Not that he would ever admit it. He complained about almost everything Conner gave him, especially if it was home cooked. But after the complaining was done, those were the meals he attacked with gusto.

Conner got into his truck and waited for Darci to back out. When she rounded the front corner of the building, she touched the brakes and slowed to a crawl. Her head was turned to the right, where two men had just stepped out the front door. They stood facing one another, both in profile. One was Wiggins. Conner didn't know the other one.

Darci did, judging from her sudden interest in what was happening. She continued up the drive, head angled that direction. When Wiggins glanced her way, she jerked her head forward and slowly picked up speed.

When Conner stepped with Kyle onto Darci's front porch an hour later, tantalizing aromas wafted to him from inside the house. Darci opened the door as the chime of the bell died away, and gave him a welcoming smile.

"Perfect timing. I just took the garlic bread out of the oven."

She motioned them inside. A living room was to his right, with a dining area to the back. A sliding glass door opened onto a patio that held a wrought-iron table and chair set. Beyond that, a privacy fence surrounded a small backyard, a swing set and slide in the center.

Kyle's eyes went right to the glass. "Can I play outside?"

"No, dinner's ready. Then it'll be dark."

Darci held up a hand. "If it's all right with you, I'll bring my laptop out after dinner and we can let them play while we work. My dad installed a great set of spotlights just for that purpose."

As soon as they were seated at the table, Kyle reached for his and Jayden's hands. But instead of starting his memorized prayer, he shot an angled glance across the table.

"I want Miss Darci to pray."

Conner tensed, ready to tell Kyle to go ahead. He would apologize to Darci later for Kyle putting her on the spot. But before he could open his mouth, Darci spoke.

"I'll be glad to."

She closed her eyes, and the words seemed to flow with no effort. She thanked God for the food and for His care and protection over them. She asked for His help through the days ahead and ended by thanking Him for new friends.

New friends. He and Kyle were those new friends. And she was thankful for them. The thought warmed him, but also left him with an unexpected longing for more.

Darci's prayer had been nice. What would he have done if Kyle had asked him instead? He'd never prayed aloud in his life. In fact, he'd never prayed, period, unless he counted those exasperated pleas for help that he'd sent skyward on a regular basis since Kyle came to stay.

Maybe he should prepare something, just in case. He hated being caught off guard. But practicing a prayer just to impress Darci somehow seemed hypocritical.

After dinner was over and the dishes were

done, she handed him her computer and pulled a file from her purse. Kyle almost ran them over getting out the door.

"Hey," he scolded, "what do you say?"

Kyle turned around with a sigh. "Excuse me."

Conner shook his head. "The kid really does have some manners. But he knows it would make me happy if he actually used them. So we're not likely to see signs of them anytime soon."

Darci flashed him a sympathetic smile. "I admire what you're doing. It's not easy raising someone else's child, especially when they seem to resent everything you do for them. Right now, he's angry at the world, and you're the easiest target. But it's going to get better."

He returned her smile with one of his own. If anything, she was perceptive. In a week and a half, she'd summed up his and Kyle's relationship to a T.

She walked out the door and slid into one of the wrought-iron chairs. "You're a good father, Conner."

He shook his head. "I'm clueless."

"We all are starting out. I've done a lot of winging it. And lots of praying."

He laid the laptop on the table and sat next to Darci. "Yeah, me too." He couldn't say he'd received any divine answers, but he'd survived thus far, and Kyle didn't seem any worse for wear. Maybe he *was* getting some help from above.

Darci opened a folder and placed it in front of him. "Here's the Marion Concrete Services file. The transactions list I printed up Saturday is in front. I've got backup for everything that's listed."

He slid the sheet to the other side of the file. Behind it was a copy of a Marion Concrete check, made payable to P. T. Aggregates. Copies of four invoices were stapled to it.

He looked over at Darci. "Anything strange about these?"

"No. They're all for loads of aggregate that went out. There's a lot of them, but that's not unusual for a large company." She flipped open her laptop. "I'm going to check them out on Sunbiz. With that keylogger, I didn't dare do it at work."

Within moments, the Division of Corporations page filled the screen. She put the company name into the search bar, then began to read. "Date filed, 2/8/11. Principal address is in Ocala. Mailing address is a PO box. Nothing surprising there." She continued to scroll. "Officer/director detail…" She let out a small gasp. "Rupert Wiggins is the president."

"It's got to be the same one. That's not a common name. Did you know he had any business interests other than his position with P. T.?"

"No."

"Who else is listed?"

She scrolled a little farther. Then her jaw dropped, and the blood drained from her face. He leaned toward her and read what was displayed. *Darci Tucker, treasurer.* The address was the same one she'd given him earlier that day.

His chest tightened. If Wiggins was going down, he fully intended to take her with him. "I need to check out the concrete company."

"How do you intend to do that?"

"I'll have a couple of my guys trade off scoping it out for a week, see if they do the amount of business that all these loads of aggregate would indicate."

She looked over at him, brows raised. "What do you mean, your guys?"

"Employees."

"Employees? You're supposed to just be a mechanic."

He smiled. "That's how I started out. Then five years ago, I bought C. S. Equipment, an equipment sales and repair company."

"I've heard of it. So how is it operating without you?"

"I've got good people in place, and I'm keeping in close contact with them." He leaned back in his chair. "Who was Wiggins talking to as we were leaving?"

"Fuller."

Ah, the slimy womanizer. "What does he do?"

"Commercial construction."

"Any connection between Fuller and Marion Concrete, other than that they both get aggregate from P. T.?"

Darci shrugged. "Maybe Fuller uses Marion for his concrete orders."

"How much aggregate does he buy?"

"Not nearly the amount Marion does. Fuller's orders come in spurts, consistent with the timing of big jobs."

"Maybe I should have someone check out Fuller Construction, too."

Darci scrolled back to the top. "Just what I thought. This was amended 11/20, last week." She heaved a sigh. "I think this started as a way to keep me from talking, but Wiggins is taking it a step further. I'm afraid it's becoming a vendetta."

A sick heaviness settled in his gut. That wasn't good.

Not at all.

Darci laid two grocery bags on the table, then hit the double switch. Light flooded the kitchen and dining area. But without Conner and Kyle, the house seemed lonely and still.

She was enjoying Conner's company more than she wanted to admit. It wasn't just the comfort of having someone to stand with her against Wiggins. It went deeper than that. Conner's presence brought to the forefront a longing that she'd buried so deep, she'd convinced herself it didn't exist.

But now that longing was making itself known every time she was alone, weaving through her heart and leaving behind a hollow emptiness that stretched all the way to her core.

She headed back toward the front door, picking up the TV remote on her way. When she pressed the power button, voices filled the room, infusing some life into her silent surroundings. She loved her little boy, but he wasn't much for conversation.

The problem was, she was getting spoiled. She and Conner and the two boys had spent most of the weekend together, as well as dinner last night. Conner had even driven back for church Sunday morning. Apparently Kyle had wanted to go with Jayden instead of where they usually attended in Chiefland. He seemed intrigued with her quiet little boy. Or maybe he just enjoyed having someone he could lead around without any argument. Whatever their relationship, Jayden didn't seem to mind.

But tonight, Conner and Kyle wouldn't be joining them. Conner had another engagement and had left her with a quick farewell in the P. T. parking lot. So she and Jayden were on their own.

She laid down the remote and stepped outside to retrieve the last of the groceries from the trunk of the Fiesta. As she straightened, two bags in each hand, a familiar vehicle crept down the road toward her. It was the gray Escalade, with Doug at the wheel. She sighed. There were worse things than being alone.

He turned into her drive, then eased to a stop. The driver door swung open and he stepped out. "You got a new car."

"No, mine's in the shop. I had a little accident."

Something dark flashed across his features. "What kind of accident?"

"Someone ran me off the road."

"Intentionally?"

"Yeah, no doubt."

Now there was no mistaking what she saw—fury, hot and pure. "Were you hurt?"

"I'm fine. What are you doing here?" She had no desire to make small talk in her driveway.

"I came to see you and Jayden." He reached out to relieve her of her burden.

She kept her grip on the bags. "You just saw us Saturday."

"I know. But that was three days ago. I miss you, Darci. I should never have listened to my stepdad."

So now he was going to place the blame for his decisions on his stepdad. He never was one to take responsibility for his mistakes. She began to walk toward the house, giving him a cold shoulder. If he was going to pop in on her any time he wished, her cozy home was going to feel like a prison.

She turned to face him on the porch. "It's all water under the bridge. Kicking yourself for past mistakes accomplishes nothing."

"You always had a good head on your shoulders." He gave her a sad smile. "Can I see Jayden for a few minutes?"

A touch of pity slipped past her defenses. Doug had always envied her home life. He had no real family of his own. Time spent with his mother had always left him frustrated, wishing he could ram some backbone into her. His dealings with his stepdad had left him beaten down and dejected.

If he wanted to see his son, she couldn't deny him that. When it came to having visits with Jayden, the law was on his side.

"All right. Come on in."

Conner wouldn't be pleased. But it wasn't as if she was inviting a stranger into her house. She walked over to where Jayden sat on the couch, an Etch A Sketch in his lap. When she tried to set it aside, he resisted her.

"Sweetheart, Doug is here to see you." She couldn't bring herself to call him *Daddy*. And until Doug insisted on it, she wasn't even going to try.

Jayden continued to stare at the toy, creating random, meandering lines.

"Jayden, look at Mommy." She lifted his chin. Several seconds later, his eyes followed. But that didn't mean she truly had his attention. Or that he was going to understand what she said.

"Let's go say hi to Doug. Okay?"

She slid the toy from his hands and picked him up. Doug stood a few feet away, his posture stiff. When she approached him, he didn't ask to hold Jayden, so she didn't offer. No matter how many times he visited, she would never shake the feeling that Jayden was nothing more than an excuse to see her.

A rattle sounded next to them and she tensed. "Did you hear that?"

"What?"

She spun toward the side wall. "It sounded like someone jimmying the window."

As soon as the words were out of her mouth, it happened again. Her gaze shot to Doug. He held a finger to his lips, then bolted out the front door. After locking it behind him, she held Jayden close and paced the floor. The blinds were all drawn, even the ones on the sliding glass door. And she'd had someone install a Charley-Bar, as well as checking all the window locks. Her house was secure. The only thing missing was a monitored alarm system. And that was more than she could afford, foreign bank accounts aside.

The minutes ticked by, and her uneasiness grew into full-blown fear. Over the past three days, she'd wished a hundred times that Doug would walk back out of her life as unexpectedly as he'd walked in. But she didn't want him hurt.

When the doorknob rattled, her pulse jumped to double time. Then a muffled voice called out. A relieved sigh escaped her mouth. It was Doug.

She opened the door, heart still pounding. "See anything?"

"Yeah, but he had too much of a head start. I think he took off as soon as he heard me open the front door."

"I'm calling the police." She picked up her cell phone. "Could you describe him?"

"I just saw him from the back. He was a short, stocky guy, but he was fast. He disappeared into the woods before I could get near him."

She relayed the information to the dispatcher, then hung up. "The police are on the way. I'm so glad you were here." She let out a relieved sigh, then had to stifle a laugh. Those were the last words she expected to say to Doug.

"I'm glad I was, too." He reached out to rest his hand on her forearm. "Let me stay. I don't want to leave you alone."

She backed away, shrugging loose from his grasp. "Thanks, but I'm fine. Everything's locked. Besides, I doubt he'll come back since you chased him off."

"Are you sure? I'm happy to stay. It's no trouble at all."

"I'm positive." She wasn't about to become

obligated to him. For men like Doug, favors came with a price.

No, if she was going to allow someone to stay and stand guard, it would be Conner.

On second thought, that wouldn't be a good idea, either.

For entirely different reasons.

SIX

Shopping bags occupied every square inch of Conner's leather sectional sofa, and an eight-foot-tall blue spruce lay in the middle of the living room floor. It was only the first Saturday in December, and the stores were already packed with people.

Darci dropped her last two bags on the couch and turned to face him. "How about plugging in a Christmas CD?"

"I don't think I have any."

She raised her brows. "Radio? We have to have Christmas music playing while we decorate. It's tradition."

He headed toward the stereo system. "If you say so."

Her tradition, maybe. He didn't have any traditions of his own. When he was growing up, how they celebrated Christmas depended on which stepfather happened to be in residence at the time.

For most of them, Christmas meant nothing more than an excuse to party. Sometimes his mom partied with them. Other times she just stayed holed up in her room with another one of her headaches—ailments he now recognized as depression.

His mom was an okay mom. At least she wasn't abusive. She just had a knack for choosing bad men. Three she married. The rest were too short-term to bother making it legal.

Conner headed to the garage to get a saw. When he returned, Kyle was removing boxes of lights and ornaments, tossing the empty plastic bags onto the floor. Before Conner could scold him, Darci picked up one of the bags and approached him. "Stuff the others in here."

Kyle gathered up what lay scattered about the floor and began to fill the bag Darci held. No argument. Probably because the request came from Darci instead of him. Or maybe it was because he was excited about Christmas.

Conner dropped to one knee and set to work trimming the trunk. Hopefully, Kyle's excitement would carry through the month. After all, he was the reason for the chaos in the living room. Conner had never been much for making a big deal over Christmas.

But since Kyle was with him, at least for

this one holiday season, he would make it the best he could for the kid. And in the process, a little bit of the Christmas cheer that seemed to be everywhere was rubbing off, chipping away at that *bah, humbug* attitude he usually carried through the entire month of December.

Kyle picked up a box of ornaments. "What goes on first?"

Darci laughed. She was kneeling in front of the window, working on assembling the tree stand. "We've got to get the tree upright before we do anything else."

After Conner cut the trunk, he and Kyle supported the tree while Darci tightened the screws to hold it in place. Jayden stood in the middle of the room, as still as a statue, watching the activity. Darci had said he could throw a temper tantrum that set her teeth on edge, complete with stomping feet and ear-piercing screams. But he hadn't seen it yet.

Darci crawled out from under the tree and stood. "Okay, I think I've got it. Let it go."

Kyle released the branches he held and danced backward to stand next to Jayden. Conner used more caution. Once sure that the tree wouldn't topple, he stepped back to view it from several different angles, then nodded his approval. "We handled that like pros."

Kyle grabbed the box of ornaments again. "Now these?"

Darci shook her head. "The lights go on first." She picked up a box and removed the hundred-count strand, snapping it free from its plastic holder. "We'll probably need all eight of these. We can't skip the back since it's standing in front of the window."

While he and Darci worked on the lights, Kyle grew more and more antsy. Finally, he plopped down on the small section of couch that wasn't still covered in decorations. "I'm bored."

Darci let the strand she was working on drape and walked over to the couch. "I have a project for you." She fished through several bags, then pulled out three packages of hooks. "How about attaching these to the ornaments so they'll be ready to hang?" After demonstrating with one, she handed him the open package of hooks.

Kyle took his assignment seriously. Over the next several minutes, he unpacked several boxes of ornaments, inserted a hook into each and laid them on the coffee table.

And he was happy doing it. In fact, Kyle would probably do anything for Darci. In two short weeks, she'd broken through his walls of anger to connect with the hurting boy beneath.

And Conner wasn't surprised. Her sweet tenderness and gentle concern would melt the coldest heart. She was a wonderful mother, just what Kyle needed. Was there maybe a chance…

What was he thinking? He didn't need to find a mother for Kyle. Conner's own mother was going to take Kyle, as soon as his stepfather regained his health. Maybe the situation wouldn't be ideal. But she couldn't do any worse than he was doing. And this newest stepfather seemed all right. At least he was a whole lot better than the ones Conner had grown up with.

Darci again joined him at the tree, and soon they had all the lights strung and plugged in. The garland went on next, and Conner smiled at Kyle. "Okay, buddy. Now we can hang those ornaments."

Kyle hurried to the table, then walked to the tree, a glass orb hanging from each hand. As he placed them, Jayden watched. Darci picked up a silver star, put the hook between his fingers and, with her hand around his, led him to the tree. As she guided the curved wire over one of the branches, she talked softly. Although Jayden didn't speak much, Darci incorporated language into everything she did.

When Conner headed back to the tree, he

turned to find the little boy's eyes on him. He extended his arm. "Do you want to hang it?"

For several moments, Jayden just watched him. His hair was a much lighter shade of brown than his mother's, but he had the same vivid blue eyes. Finally, one side of his mouth cocked up in the slightest smile, and he reached for the hook.

Conner steadied a branch. "Let's hang it right here."

Whether Jayden understood his words or his actions, Conner wasn't sure. But within seconds, the miniature bell was hanging exactly as he'd intended. He straightened to find Darci watching him, a softness in her eyes.

After Kyle placed the last ornament, Conner closed the blinds, blocking out the midafternoon sun, and dimmed the overhead lights. Then he sat back to admire their handiwork, arms outstretched on the back of the couch and an ankle crossed over his knee.

Kyle was almost dancing with excitement. "Now we need presents to put under it."

Conner laughed. The kid probably knew that most of them would have his name on them. "Those are coming."

"Will Miss Darci and Jayden have presents, too?"

"I'm sure they will."

"Here?"

Conner hesitated, warmth filling him at the thought of shopping for Darci. The act somehow seemed intimate. He hadn't thought that far ahead, but yes, he would definitely buy a gift for Darci. "There'll be presents for Jayden and Miss Darci under the tree, too."

Kyle seemed satisfied and quickly shifted gears. "Can Jayden spend the night tonight?"

Darci put a hand on Kyle's shoulder. "He's a little young to spend the night away from home. But you'll see each other tomorrow."

"Where are we going?"

He and Darci answered simultaneously, "Church."

Initially, he'd started attending for Kyle, not believing Christianity had any real relevance for his own life. But something had changed over the past few weeks. Some of it was due to the messages he'd heard at the Chiefland and Cedar Key churches. Some of it was due to watching the gradual change in Kyle's behavior. But seeing that faith lived out in Darci's life had affected him in a way that was hard to ignore.

Darci eased onto the couch next to him, and he dropped his arm to let it rest across her shoulders.

"Thank you."

"For what?"

He nodded toward the tree. "All this."

"You're the one who bought everything. I just helped set it up."

"You did more than that. When you climbed into my truck this morning, you brought the spirit of Christmas with you."

Before she could respond, Kyle crawled up onto the couch next to her.

"Great job." She held up a hand for a high five, which Kyle vigorously returned. "Our tree could win first place in a World's Best Decorated Christmas Tree contest."

Jayden reached for her, and she pulled him onto her lap. And the four of them sat nestled together. Hundreds of tiny bulbs cast their light throughout the room while Perry Como crooned, "There's no place like home for the holidays."

Conner released a sigh, an odd sense of contentment seeping into every cell in his body. Darci had said *our tree*. What would it be like to have someone share his life, to think in terms of *ours* instead of *mine*? To have his very own family?

He mentally shook himself. Kyle was only temporary. His stepdad wouldn't be able to milk a heart attack forever.

Actually, Darci was temporary, too. He'd

been forewarned. She didn't do relationships. Her focus was 100 percent on her son. Once this was over, he would head back to C. S. Equipment, and she would continue at P. T. Maybe they would remain friends. He hoped so. But that would be all.

And it was for the best. Any future with Darci would involve fatherhood, something he had no business even considering. He didn't have what it took to be a good husband, much less a good father. And having grown up with no real example of either, he wasn't likely to learn, with or without God's help.

All the arguments against falling for Darci were right on the tip of his tongue, backed up by the voice of reason.

Unfortunately, his heart was ignoring them.

Darci made her way toward home under a steel-gray sky, the heavy cloud cover creating the illusion of dusk. The rain would probably start soon and continue through the night, followed by a cold front.

But the weekend had been perfect. And not just the weather. Shopping with Conner had been fun. Helping him decorate while Christmas carols played in the background had provided a temporary balm for the loneliness that had begun to plague her life.

Then yesterday, Conner and Kyle had again joined them for church. Once she and her friend Allison had exited the platform after singing in the worship ensemble, the eight of them had occupied an entire row—she and Conner and the boys, Allison and her husband, and Hunter and his wife.

Darci sighed. All her closest friends had found their happily-ever-afters. Allison married Blake, and a year later, Hunter met Meagan and fell in love. Darci was the last holdout.

Of course, she would be holding out for a long time, no matter what she felt for Conner. Once Kyle went back to live with Conner's mom and stepdad, Conner would again be free. She refused to saddle him with a child, especially one like Jayden. It wouldn't be fair to Conner, and it wouldn't be fair to Jayden. No, her special little boy was her responsibility, hers and hers alone.

She pressed the brake, then turned onto Highway 19-98. Today at work, she'd discovered an icon in the right-hand portion of her task bar—a blue circle with three white dots. Maybe it was nothing. Maybe it had always been there, and she'd just never noticed. But chances were good someone had added it recently.

Her first thought had been the keylogger

program. But when she clicked the icon, she landed on a website. She immediately clicked back off. If Wiggins was watching, he would assume she'd gone there by accident. But in that brief moment, she'd gotten what she needed.

The site was LogMeIn. She wasn't sure what LogMeIn did, but she would find out tonight. In fact, she and Conner could work on it together. He would be about forty-five minutes behind her.

A half mile from home, she glanced in her rearview mirror, something she did regularly now. Doug was behind her. She heaved a sigh. She would let him see Jayden, then send him on his way.

She turned onto her street, and when she reached her driveway, movement at the side of the house drew her attention. A figure stood there, dressed in all black, a ski mask hiding his face. He turned toward her, then bolted away, headed toward the woods that bordered the backs of the houses.

Panic shot through her. Her mom and Jayden were inside. She screeched to a stop next to her mother's Intrepid.

Doug apparently saw the man, too. Without taking the time to turn into the drive, he jammed on the brakes at the edge of her yard, half on and half off the road. Before she could even get out of the car, he was in hot pursuit.

Leaving Doug to his business, she snatched her purse and ran to the door. When she stepped inside, her mother looked up from the book she'd been reading to Jayden and raised her brows.

"Are you all right, dear?"

Darci smoothed her hair with shaking fingers. Her mom was oblivious to the fact that moments earlier, there had been a masked man just outside the dining room window.

Before she could explain, Doug appeared at the still-open front door, breathing heavily. His jaw was tight, and there was a somberness in his eyes that sent uneasiness through her.

"Darci, you'd better look at this."

The ominous tone confirmed what she saw in his gaze, and suddenly, she didn't want to know what he had found.

Her mother set the book aside and stood. "Honey?"

Darci held up a hand. "Stay here with Jayden. I'll be right back."

She dropped her purse on the end table and followed Doug off the porch and around the side of the house.

"I lost him." Doug threw the words over his shoulder. "It may have been the same guy who was trying to get in your window last week. But this is what I wanted you to see."

He stopped at the dining room window and pointed to the ground. At the edge of the shrubs that lined the foundation of the house was a six-inch-long pipe, a metal cap on each end. A thick string emerged from a small hole in the center.

"What is it?" It looked sinister.

"I think it's a pipe bomb. I'd say your prowler dropped it before he had a chance to ignite it." He nailed her with a stern gaze. "You need to level with me, Darci. Who is after you?"

Wiggins? No, if he wanted to kill her with a bomb, he would plant it in her car. A wave of nausea rolled through her at this new possibility. *Oh, God, help me.*

She closed her eyes and shook her head. "I don't know."

"You must know something. This is serious stuff."

She turned without responding "I'm calling the police." When she reached the corner of the house, she stopped and looked back at Doug. "Don't mention the pipe bomb in front of my mom. I don't want her to worry."

"All right. But I need to make sure you're safe."

She walked away without comment. She

didn't want Doug's protection. She'd gotten along fine without him for the past five years. But she would face that argument later.

When she got back inside, she pulled her phone from her purse and addressed her mother. "Someone was prowling around the yard, hanging out next to the dining room window. I'm going to have the police check it out, just to be safe."

Her mom's eyes filled with concern. "Oh, my. Are you going to be okay? I can stay with you."

"No, you go on. But maybe you could keep Jayden at your place for a few days."

"I'll be glad to. Why don't you come home, too?"

Darci hesitated. It was tempting. But she wouldn't put her parents in danger. And as long as they had Jayden, he would be out of harm's way, too.

"I'll be fine. I've got good, strong locks."

Her mother gave a reluctant nod, then turned to Doug. "Will you stay with her until the police get here?"

"Yes, ma'am, I'll be glad to."

Darci sighed and placed her call. By the time she'd finished, her mom had packed a bag for Jayden. Darci scooped him up and gave him a tight squeeze, breathing in the berry scent that still lingered from last night's bath. She was going to miss her little boy. She'd never been separated from him for more than one night.

After she put him down, her mother took his hand and opened the front door. Before stepping onto the porch, she threw Darci one more worried glance. "Are you sure you're going to be okay?"

Doug put a hand on her shoulder. "I'll take care of her, ma'am."

She bristled and followed her mom and little boy out the door. Before putting Jayden into his car seat, she gave him one more hug. Then she stood waving as the car backed and moved up the road. Her mom waved back. Jayden didn't. His head rested against the side of his car seat, his gaze straight ahead.

She turned and walked back inside. When Doug put his hand on her shoulder, she shrugged it off.

He heaved an exasperated sigh. "Darci, let me help you. Whoever is after you, he's playing for keeps. Come and stay with me."

She faced him squarely. "I'm not staying with you, so you need to let it go. I appreciate your concern, and I won't keep Jayden from you, but that's the extent of it."

Music sounded from inside her purse and grew in volume. She pushed past Doug, grabbed her phone and swiped the screen. It was Conner. He had picked up the chicken and the yellow rice packet they had talked about and wanted to know if she needed anything else.

"No, that'll do it. I've got plenty of stuff for a salad. But there's a change of plans. It's going to be just you and me and Kyle. I sent Jayden with my mother."

"Is everything okay?" There was a distinct note of concern in Conner's tone. Though she'd tried to keep her own nonchalant, he was intuitive enough to know something was wrong.

"I got home from work, and someone was in my yard. I'll tell you about it when you get here."

When she ended the call, Doug was studying her with his arms crossed. "Who was that?"

"Conner." Not that it was any of his business.

"Who is Conner?"

"A…friend." Let him think there was more between them than there actually was. Then maybe he would leave her alone.

Doug uncrossed his arms, and his hands curled into fists. Gone was the easygoing, smooth-talking man she'd fallen in love with in college. Anger flashed in his eyes. But it was tinged with desperation, which didn't make sense. Doug didn't know the meaning of the word *desperate*. He could schmooze his way into or out of anything.

Except this, because she wasn't budging.

"Fine," he began. "I had hoped that the three of us could be a family, you and me and Jayden. I'm willing to give you one more chance. Otherwise, tomorrow I see my lawyer."

Her mouth suddenly went dry. "For what?"

"Custody of Jayden."

Her heart stuttered, and her thoughts spun off in a thousand different directions. No, not Jayden. He was her life. Doug had no interest in him. It was obvious every time he saw him. This afternoon, he never once directed his attention to his son. So what was he trying to accomplish?

"Is this about child support? If so, you don't need to worry. I've supported him by myself for four years. I'm not going to come after you."

Doug laughed, but there was no humor in the sound. "Do you really think a little child support would put a dent in my financial position?"

No, it probably wouldn't. His family had money, lots of it. She remembered that from their college days. He had the rich family, and she had the loving one. And he had envied her for it.

Was that what this was about, a yearning for a family of his own? But why now, when her world was falling down around her and her life was spinning out of control?

Sirens sounded in the distance, moving closer. The police would be there within minutes. Doug would have to give a report. Then he would be free to leave.

She put some force behind her words. "Do what you feel you need to. We're over."

"Have it your way." There was an iciness in his tone that she'd never heard before. He walked out the door, shutting it behind him a little harder than necessary.

She was a good mother. Surely the courts wouldn't take custody away from her and give it to Doug, no matter how much money he had.

A new thought shot through her mind, almost bringing her to her knees.

If she didn't find a way out of the web that Wiggins was weaving around her, it wouldn't be her parents raising Jayden.

It would be Doug.

Conner ran a comb through his wet hair, then stepped from the bathroom, once again feeling human. There were still faint traces of grease staining his cuticles, but that was how it would be as long as he was at P. T.

And he wasn't complaining. The same as a month ago, he was right where he wanted to be. Except his focus had shifted from getting justice for Claire to protecting Darci. That was why several changes of women's clothes now occupied the closet in the room next to Kyle's, and ladies' toiletries had been added to the little-boy stuff in the hall bath. Last night had been the final straw. If Darci had gotten home a little later, she and Jayden could have been seriously hurt.

She hadn't wanted to stay with him. In fact, she'd put up a valiant fight. She believed that Wiggins was just trying to scare her, not kill her, at least for now. And she insisted that her house was secure, even promised to look into getting an alarm system.

But her biggest argument had been about Kyle—she didn't want to put him in danger. Actually, Conner didn't, either. So today he had hired a bodyguard. The guy was massive. He had a good three or four inches over Conner's own six feet and outweighed him by at least seventy-five pounds. And if that wasn't enough, the dude was carrying a Glock on one hip and a SIG on the other. He was currently somewhere outside, making his rounds.

Halfway to the living room, the doorbell rang. He tensed, then instantly relaxed. No one was getting past Goliath out there.

After checking the peephole, he swung open the door. His bodyguard held a box that bore a well-known logo.

"Did you order something from Amazon?"

"I did. But it's a little late for the UPS guy, isn't it?" It was almost seven o'clock.

"That's what I told him. But he said with the Christmas rush, it was taking him longer to get through his route."

Conner took the package and closed the door. Although he'd ordered several items for Kyle's Christmas gifts, he knew what was in this small, flat box. He'd bought him a Bible. He should have bought one for himself at the same time, but there were too many options. Darci could probably give him some advice.

He moved to the desk that sat off the side of the living room and tore open the box. With the abundance of gifts that would be arriving over the next two weeks, he was probably going to end up spoiling the kid. But this first Christmas without his mother, Conner couldn't seem to stop himself. At least this gift was a practical one that would be with Kyle long after the last toy was lost or broken.

Conner pulled the book from its package.

The Complete Illustrated Children's Bible was printed across the top of the colorful cover. Inside, full-page illustrations brought the stories to life. He skimmed the creation story, then thumbed through several pages. The Christmas story would be in there somewhere. Someone who knew the Bible would know right where to look. He didn't. When it came to what was inside this book, he didn't know much more than Kyle did.

But they could learn together. The thought of sitting on the couch, reading the stories aloud with Kyle tucked in next to him seared a path to his heart. Maybe he shouldn't wait till Christmas. Kyle would probably be back with his grandparents by then, and Conner would miss the opportunity.

He closed the book and put it back in the box. As he pushed himself to his feet, his phone rang, and the name of his parts manager stretched across the screen. Since the beginning of last week, Conner had had four guys trading off watching activity at both Fuller Construction and Marion Concrete. Rusty was assigned to oversee it.

"You got news?"

"The construction company does a pretty brisk business. It all looks on the up-and-up."

Conner nodded. Fuller. He'd hoped to hear the opposite. "And what about Marion Concrete?"

"All last week and yesterday, nothing. Finally, one truck went out with fresh concrete today."

Interesting. "We'll keep an eye on them a little longer. But forget about Fuller."

When Conner stepped into the living room, Kyle sat on the couch, game controller in hand. Darci was next to him with her computer on her lap.

Conner nodded toward the big-screen TV, currently lit up by weapons fire. "Is that racket bothering you?"

Darci smiled. "Not at all." She raised both hands in the air and stretched. "Dinner should be out in twenty minutes."

He drew in a fragrant breath. It was only frozen lasagna, but the way his stomach was rumbling, they might as well have been in some fancy Italian restaurant.

Kyle put the controller on the couch and sprang to his feet. "Uncle Conner, I know what I want you to get me for Christmas. One thing, anyway."

Conner sank onto the couch next to Darci. "Oh, yeah?"

"I have to show you." He ran from the living room, down the hall toward his bedroom. A minute later, he returned clutching a sale flyer from a toy store, apparently confiscated from the mail. After spreading it out on the coffee table, he pointed to the page. "Here."

Conner leaned forward. Kyle had circled the item he pointed out, along with two others. "Hmm, the Millennium Falcon. You know, that's a model. It would have to be put together."

"You could help me."

Conner smiled. The fact that Kyle wanted to spend time building *anything* with him meant things were looking up. "I could. Your uncle Conner is a pretty experienced model builder. I did a lot of these when I was a kid." It kept him in his room and out of the way of the adults in the house, which was usually to his advantage.

He folded the flyer. "Leave this with me, and I'll see what I can do."

"I'm not finished with it yet. I might want some other things." He scooped it up and ran back to his room.

"You're doing a good job with him."

He frowned. When he looked over at her, she was studying him with those big blue eyes. There was sadness in their depths.

"Why won't you believe me?"

"I have no idea what it takes to be a good father."

"What was yours like?"

He gave a snort. "Which one?"

"I'm sorry. My parents have been married for thirty years. I don't even know what it's like to not have a stable home."

"My real dad left when I was five. The main thing I remember about him was his temper. I was able to avoid him most of the time, but Claire had a rebellious streak he never was able to beat out of her."

He sighed. "The next one mostly ignored me. Fortunately for me, he didn't like little boys. Unfortunately for Claire, he liked little girls. She never told anyone until a couple of months before she disappeared."

Kyle reappeared and plopped down on the couch, ready to resume his game. Although the interruption gave Darci no opportunity to respond, she shot him a glance filled with sympathy. Conner's gaze went to her laptop screen.

"What are you working on?"

"Something I was going to do last night but never got to." She angled the screen so he could see it better. "Yesterday, I noticed an icon on my task bar that I hadn't seen before, LogMeIn. It allows you to access a computer remotely."

"So what is that?" He nodded toward the screen. It looked like vendor information for Marion Concrete Services.

"My computer at work. I used my email, along with the password Wiggins set up for those two files, and it took me right to my desktop."

Uneasiness trickled over him. "Are you sure the keylogger isn't picking up what you're doing?"

"I haven't really done anything except type in my name and password for the accounting program. Everything else has been clicks."

He frowned. "That doesn't mean anything. Some keyloggers just pick up keystrokes, but others will do a screenshot with each mouse click."

Her brows drew together, creating fine vertical lines. As long as the clicks weren't recorded, she should be safe. Unless Wiggins checked the time that she logged in to her accounting program.

She ended the session then brought up the log-in screen again. "There's one computer that probably doesn't have a keylogger installed." Her fingers flew over the keys as she typed in an email address. "I got this from the Marion Concrete Services vendor information."

She tried the same password, and another desktop filled the screen. Her breath whooshed out. "This is Marion Concrete's computer." She looked over at him, her eyes wide. "Why does Wiggins want it to look like I have access to it?"

"Because there's something fishy there, and he wants to pin it on you."

She made a few clicks. "QuickBooks, the same program I have at work. Vendors, customers, it's all here." She turned toward him, her eyes lit with excitement. "Do you realize what an opportunity this is? I can see everything. Wiggins set it up so if things came crashing down, he could pin it on me. But I'm sure he didn't intend for us to actually see this. We've outsmarted him."

She turned her attention back to the computer and brought up the list of vendors. There were ten, one of which was P. T. Aggregates. She clicked on each of them, scrolling through their payment history. "We have the utility company, a couple of credit cards, a gas card, insurance and a couple of equipment vendors. What they pay to P. T. seems consistent with what I invoice. It's a lot of aggregate, but if they do big business, it would be justifiable."

But from what Rusty had just told him, they didn't do big business.

Darci clicked on Customers. Several were listed, all of them construction companies. According to the accounts receivable activity, they all purchased concrete on a regular basis.

She exited QuickBooks, then logged off. "Everything looks legit, but the numbers could have been doctored."

Conner nodded. "I think my next step is having a talk with Jerry."

"The scale operator?"

"Yep. He sees the tickets. He would know whenever a truck is headed to Marion Concrete. If there are loads being invoiced by P. T. that aren't going out and concrete deliveries being invoiced by Marion that aren't being made, I'd say we have a shell corporation set up for laundering money."

Darci's shoulders slumped. "And I'm the treasurer."

He put his arm around her and pulled her to his side. "We're going to find a way to clear you. We've just got to keep you safe in the meantime."

As he said the words, a shadow darkened the edges of his mind, a danger he hadn't yet put a name to. Wiggins would see Darci's login. That in itself wouldn't be a problem. It was expected.

But if he looked at the time, he would think she came back to the office after hours. Or he would know she accessed it through LogMeIn.

The uneasiness grew stronger. Was there

a way to tell when someone had used the program? Did it keep a record of log-ins?

Darci started to close her laptop, but Conner held up a hand.

"Log back in to the Marion Concrete account. I need to check something."

"Okay." There was a question in her tone, but she did as he asked.

He studied the screen. "Click on Dashboard."

Details appeared, and his stomach filled with lead. He pointed to the bottom right. "Most recent accesses. It shows someone was logged on tonight from 6:22 to 6:36 p.m. I'm guessing the host name listed there is my IP address."

Darci gasped, her eyes wide. "Wiggins will know it was me."

"If he looks. Maybe he won't."

But he didn't believe his own words. As closely as Wiggins was watching her, he would see it eventually. It was just a matter of time.

He pulled her closer, thankful that she was with him instead of alone at her house.

And doubly thankful for the monster of a man standing guard outside.

SEVEN

The roar of the Sea Ray's motor filled the air as it accelerated out of the channel. Its nose rose, and it surged forward, parting the waves with little effort. Darci tipped back her head, relishing the wind in her hair and the sun on her face. Layers of tension peeled away and dropped off into the wake fanning out behind Blake's boat.

Conner's arm went around her, and she opened her eyes to smile at him. They were huddled together on the forward-facing part of the L-shaped seat, Hunter and Meagan at the other end. Kyle and Jayden were crowded into the corner, wearing thick orange life jackets. Blake captained the boat, with Allison in the rear-facing seat next to him. It was a tight squeeze, getting all eight of them on, but the close quarters didn't seem to be dimming anyone's spirits.

She released a contented sigh. This outing

was just what she'd needed. Besides the desire to get away, she missed her little boy so much it hurt. Conner had protested, wanting to keep her under lock and key for the weekend, the bodyguard a short distance away. The only thing that had convinced him was the fact that she would have unofficial police escort the entire time. Hunter was armed and so was Blake, a former law enforcement officer himself.

So she was determined to relax and not let anything spoil what promised to be a wonderful day. The cold front earlier in the week had already fizzled out, leaving them with temperatures in the low seventies. Besides the perfect weather, she was surrounded by some of her favorite people.

She looked over at the boys. Kyle's eyes shone with excitement, and a grin stretched across his face. Jayden even wore a soft half smile.

A short time later, Blake circled around to head toward Seahorse Key, where they had planned a picnic lunch. After dropping the front anchor and backing as close to shore as possible, he killed the engine and moved to the rear of the boat. Soon he and Hunter had the back anchor set on the beach. Behind them, the Seahorse Key lighthouse peeked over the tops of the trees.

Conner stepped onto the swim platform and lowered himself into the water while Darci removed Jayden's life jacket. Kyle had peeled his off the instant the boat stopped and stood on the platform almost dancing.

Conner held up a hand. "Hold on, buddy. I'm going to help Miss Darci down first."

After kicking off her sandals, she stepped from the platform to the first step and drew in a sharp breath. The air temperature was a comfortable seventy degrees, but almost two weeks before Christmas, the water was cold. Fortunately, it was only knee-deep. For Conner, anyway. For her it would be closer to midthigh. For the boys, wading ashore wasn't an option, not this time of year.

She made her way down the swim ladder, Conner's hand at her back, then planted her feet on the sandy bottom. When she reached for Jayden, he drew back. He'd been on a boat only a handful of times and wasn't much for trying new things.

Before she could coax him toward her, Kyle put a gentle hand on his back and eased him forward. "We're going to play on the beach. It'll be fun."

Darci wrapped her hands around his waist and lifted him down. Conner did the same with Kyle, and they made the twenty-foot trek to shore. As soon as Kyle's tennis shoes met the sand, he reached for Jayden's hand and led him down the beach.

Conner called after them, "Hold on. We're going to eat lunch first."

Allison shifted the blanket she held and waved them off. "Let them expend some of that pent-up energy. We'll get everything laid out while you're gone."

The boys continued their jaunt down the beach until a downed tree drew Kyle's interest. He released Jayden's hand and stepped onto the trunk, then made his way along its length, arms extended.

Darci drew to a stop, Conner next to her. When he spoke, his tone was low.

"He's a different kid from what he was just a month ago."

She nodded. She'd noticed the change herself. "He's adjusting. Like I told you, you're doing a good job with him."

Conner shook his head. "Until I met you, he was still the same angry boy that came to live with me five months earlier. So my parenting skills, what little I have, have nothing to do with it. It's you and Jayden that have made the difference." He reached for her hand and entwined his fingers with hers.

Her heart swelled, from his touch as much

as his words. Several times, he'd given her an encouraging sideways hug or draped his arm across the back of the couch as she sat next to him, letting it rest on her shoulders. Those gestures had always felt casual.

Like on the boat. He had his arm around her the entire ride. But there hadn't been much choice. There wasn't room to sit shoulder to shoulder.

But this was different. He was reaching out to her, connecting with her. And as she stood with her hand tucked into his, a sense of expectancy enveloped her, the feeling that their relationship was a hairsbreadth away from evolving into something beyond mere friendship.

Before she could ponder further, Kyle jumped down from the tree trunk and ran up to grasp Conner's other hand.

"I'm hungry."

Conner smiled. "Then we'd better get back."

Darci snagged Jayden's hand. Then the four of them walked down the beach, all abreast. Conner didn't release her, even when they rounded the bend and came into view of the others.

Meagan smiled up at them from where she knelt on one of two blankets spread out on the sand. Allison was next to her, the two of them distributing individually wrapped deli sandwiches. Blake tore open a large bag of chips, and Hunter pulled drinks from a cooler. Beyond them, a flock of seagulls waited for whatever morsels might get left behind.

Meagan's gaze went to their joined hands, and her smile widened. She probably thought she was getting her wish—the two of them a couple. She was a little premature. A lot of issues stood in the way, some of them insurmountable.

Kyle released Conner's hand and ran to stand in the middle of the nearest blanket. "Come on, you guys. This one's for our family."

Darci's heart stuttered. *Our family.* That was what they would look like to anyone who saw them—a husband and wife with their two children. Longing carved a hollow trail through her heart.

She sank down next to Kyle, and Conner and Jayden followed. As Hunter blessed the food, two hands gripped hers, one large and one tiny. Kyle completed the circle of four.

A family. Someday it would have to end. But today she would enjoy the illusion. She wouldn't focus on the loneliness sure to bombard her when Conner and Kyle were no longer part of her life. And she wouldn't think about the impact it would have on Kyle when his grandparents took him back. Yet another upheaval in his short life.

That sad, angry boy had woven his way right into her heart. So had his kind and caring uncle. Almost from the start, she and Conner had shared a special bond.

She would cherish it while it lasted. And when it was over...well, she would face that when the time came.

And not a moment before.

Darci stepped through the break room door into the noonday sunshine. Her small cooler hung over one shoulder, her purse over the other. Today lunch would be in her car. Conner had sent her a text shortly after ten this morning, telling her to call when she got a chance. Whatever he wanted to talk to her about, they probably wouldn't want Wiggins eavesdropping.

After unlocking her car, she tossed her cooler and purse over the console and slid into the driver's seat. She finally had her Corolla back. She'd gotten the call yesterday morning that it was ready. So after work, Conner had followed her to return the rental car and taken her to the body shop. The whole situation had been a little inconvenient, but at least she'd gotten a new paint job for her trouble.

She removed her sandwich and apple from her cooler and unscrewed the cap on her water bottle. After tearing open the small bag of chips, she pulled her phone from her purse and dialed Conner. "Hey, what's up?"

He got right to the point. "I talked to Jerry, and one load of aggregate goes out to Marion Concrete once every week or two. Someone's creating fake tickets."

"That doesn't surprise me. Now we need to figure out why."

"That's not all. The bulldozer has been here for years."

Darci wrinkled her brow. He was losing her. "What bulldozer?"

"The Case."

"That's impossible. I've got a copy of the cashier's check and everything. Before April of this year, that piece of equipment doesn't show up on the depreciation schedule, the book asset detail or anything."

"Then what you're looking at has been doctored."

"How did you find this out?" Maybe his information was faulty.

"One of the equipment operators, Joe Samson. During our morning break, I was asking him about some of the equipment. I wondered if P. T. was going to be replacing any of the older pieces, because we've got some expensive repairs coming up. He didn't think so. I said that the Case probably blew this year's budget. That's when he told me it wasn't bought this year. When he came to P. T. five years ago, it was already here."

She shook her head, confusion swirling inside her. What was purchased with that $40,000 check? Apparently it wasn't the Case. "I'll see what I can figure out."

"Be careful. Don't do anything on your computer."

She took a bite of her ham-and-cheese sandwich and talked around it. "I can look at the depreciation schedules. I deal with those all the time."

Although Conner finally agreed, his tone held reluctance. "Just don't take any unnecessary chances."

"I won't. But I'm hoping I'll have some news when I meet you out here at five."

She said farewell then dialed her mother. Last night, she'd had a long conversation with her. It wasn't fair to expect her to keep Jayden and not level with her. Besides that, her mom was a praying lady. And right now, Darci could use all the prayers she could get.

At her request, her mom put Jayden on the phone. Only two days had passed since Saturday's outing, and already the separation was killing her.

"Hi, sweetie, it's Mommy." She injected enthusiasm into her tone. "Are you being a good boy for Grandma?"

There was no answer. She didn't expect any.

When her mom came back on the phone, her tone was filled with worry. "Please stay safe."

"That's my plan. I'm a lot safer with Conner than staying alone. He's even hired a bodyguard."

"He seems like such a nice young man. A much better choice than Doug was."

Darci shook her head. She'd told her mom last Saturday that she and Conner were nothing more than friends. Her mom had just nodded with a knowing half smile. Whatever she thought she knew, she was seeing things that weren't there.

After finishing her conversation with her mother, she dropped her apple core into the cooler and stepped out of the car. Once inside her office, she sat down at the computer. There was nothing in the equipment file that would show what really happened. She'd already looked.

Of course, she'd checked the depreciation schedule, too. As expected, the Case was added in April. She'd even gone back to the prior year, and there was no mention of it, fully depreciated or not. And it wasn't on the book asset detail, either.

But she hadn't gone back any further than that. Somewhere in the past, that 2006 Case bulldozer had to be in the records. Unless Joe was mistaken.

She clicked on a folder titled *Depreciation Schedules*. There was one for every year, going all the way back to 2004 when the mine opened. She would start with 2006 and work her way forward.

She brought the cursor over the file, but just before clicking on it, she hesitated. The date modified was May 31…of the current year. In fact, each depreciation schedule from 2006 through last year was modified in May.

Right after Claire found the irregularity on the bank statement.

Her eyes widened. Someone made off with almost $40,000, and when Claire figured it out, they created backup for an equipment purchase that never took place and wiped out all traces of the original one.

Movement in her peripheral vision drew her attention. Wiggins stood in her doorway. She jumped and clicked off the folder.

"You startled me. I was getting ready to work on depreciation entries. The John Deere

410G backhoe is going to be fully depreciated next month, so I've got to redo my cal-
culations."

Wiggins crossed his arms. "That won't be
necessary. I've decided I don't need you anymore."

Her jaw went slack, and her thoughts scattered. "You're firing me?"

"Firing, letting go, laying off, however you
want to put it. Pack up your things and leave."

She shook her head, her mind still spinning.
"You can't do this. I'm going to Peter Turlong."
It was an empty threat. Turlong had hired her,
but he'd left everything in Wiggins's hands,
including the hiring of new employees and the
firing of current ones.

Wiggins stepped into her office and closed
the door behind him. "Don't threaten me,
Tucker. I can bury you. I think you've figured
that out." His voice was low, ensuring that his
words wouldn't carry beyond her office walls.
But it held a lethal coldness. "If you want to be
around to raise the boy of yours, you'd better
gather your things and leave quietly."

Before she could formulate a response, he
opened the door and disappeared down the
hall.

She dropped her head into her hands, the
full weight of her situation bearing down on

her. She was jobless. But that wasn't her biggest concern. Without her work at P. T., she'd never be able to clear her name.

Why was he firing her now? It had to be about more than the depreciation folder. He'd accessed the LogMeIn activity log.

She slid the two pictures of Jayden into her purse, retrieved her cooler from the closet and flipped her sweater over her arm. That was pretty much it. Once she left, she would text Conner and ask him to call her on his afternoon break. Since he had ridden with her, she would need to pick him up. But she would have him meet her at the road. If Wiggins didn't know that the two of them had contact outside of work, she wasn't going to broadcast it to him. Maybe Conner could continue trying to clear her.

She made her way through the break room and out the back door, thankful that she didn't encounter anyone along the way. Having to explain she'd just been let go would add humiliation to her despair. She'd never been fired from a job. She'd never even been reprimanded.

After stepping out the door, she made her way toward her car. As she got closer, dread bore down on her. Her passenger door was slightly ajar. Someone had broken in to her car.

She picked up her pace, closing the final

yards at a jog. The window was whole, but the rubber around it was warped in one spot. Someone had used a Slim Jim or similar tool to gain access. Nothing inside looked disturbed. Her stereo system was even still there.

Then she saw it—a black duffel bag on the front passenger floorboard.

She backed away, shaking her head. Fear slid down her throat and settled in her stomach like lead. She needed to call the police. It could be a bomb.

Or it could be something Wiggins had planted to get her arrested. She needed to find out what the bag contained before bringing in law enforcement.

She crept back to the car and opened the door. She wouldn't pick up the bag. She would just carefully open the zipper and peek inside. Then she would decide where to go from there.

Leaning into the car, she dropped her sweater and cooler into the seat and reached for the zipper. A phone had slid between the seat and the bag, its edge barely visible. Was it dropped accidentally or planted there? She grasped the zipper and pulled it back one tooth at a time. As the bag fell open, her stomach went into a free fall. It contained bundles of money.

Dear God, no. More evidence against her.

Physical evidence, right in her car. She needed to get rid of it, but not leave behind any prints. The thought went against everything honest in her. But what choice did she have?

She straightened and looked around her. Her purse still hung from her left shoulder, her phone inside. But before she could call Conner, the knob twisted and the break room door started to swing open. Instinctively, she pushed her car door shut and ducked.

Wiggins's voice drifted to her. "That's hers there, the red Toyota."

Her pulse began to race. Wiggins was with someone. And he was talking about *her*.

Staying in a crouch, she duck walked around the back of the SUV next to her and peered beneath. Although she hadn't heard the second person speak, there were two sets of feet, and they were moving toward her car. Who was Wiggins with?

As they passed the vehicle she was hiding behind, she crawled to the next.

Wiggins continued, "She knows I've been watching her. She probably suspected that we were closing in on her and planned to take off. But her car's still here, so she's got to be hiding nearby."

"I'll call in backup." The voice belonged to the other man. He continued, no longer talking to Wiggins. After relaying details, he requested more units, ending with the suggestion that they send a couple of K-9s. "In the meantime, I'll keep an eye on her car. Without transportation, she won't get far."

She swallowed hard against the bile rising in her throat. The other man was a cop, someone Wiggins had called. And she was their suspect. Within minutes, the property would be crawling with deputies. But if she could get enough of a head start...

She crawled past several other vehicles, moving toward the woods. But between her and safety lay the stretch of asphalt that held the two picnic tables. She would never be able to pass through it unseen.

As she reached the last vehicle, Wiggins's voice stopped her. "Hey, look what she left behind."

Anticipation coursed through her. Wiggins had seen the bag. Of course, he was probably the one who had put it there, or had someone put it there. For the next several seconds, both men would be focused on that bag.

She pulled off her shoes, straightened and ran barefoot the final fifteen feet, clutching her purse to her side. After slipping around the corner of the building, she covered the final thirty feet.

Inside the forest, dried pine needles and twigs crunched beneath her feet, digging into the tender skin of her soles. She slipped back into her dress shoes, then resumed her panicked dash. If the men heard her, they would come after her. She prayed that the breeze rustling the trees would be enough to mask the noise she was making.

Because she couldn't slow down, even for a moment. She had to put as much distance as possible between her and the authorities now descending on P. T. And the dogs. She would have to somehow elude the dogs.

For several minutes, she ran, panic pounding close on her heels. Her lungs burned, and perspiration ran down her sides and back. She had no destination in mind, no thought for where she would spend the night. The fight-or-flight response had kicked in. And she was in full-blown flight.

Her toe caught a root, and the ground rose up to meet her. She slammed forward face-first, the bed of pine needles doing nothing to cushion her fall. After several moments, she pushed herself to an upright position. Her purse had landed three feet away, its contents strewn about the forest floor. Her left hip hurt, likely bruised from a tree root. And needles of pain shot through her left shoulder and wrist.

She rubbed the complaining joints, then made a couple of circles with her hand and a wider one with her arm. Everything seemed to work.

But she had no clue where she was. For ten or fifteen minutes, she'd run blindly. The road should be to her left, but she had no idea how far.

She needed to get her head on straight. Not only were the cops after her, but Wiggins's men likely were, too.

And she had nowhere to turn. Her parents would be watched. So would all her friends on Cedar Key. And there was too much of a chance that someone would be keeping an eye on Conner, too. Maybe she could call Doug.

She dismissed the idea as soon as it crossed her mind. She didn't trust him, even less since he'd threatened to fight her for custody of Jayden. If she was going to bring Doug into her confidence, she may as well hand Jayden over to him now.

Hopelessness descended on her. She was on her own, alone in the woods in a pair of dress pants, a silk blouse and a light sweater. And nothing to eat or drink except a protein bar and a minibottle of water that she carried in case of emergency. When she'd put them in her purse, this wasn't the kind of emergency she'd had in mind.

No, she wouldn't give up. God gave her a brain. She would use it. If she conserved, she could make the water and protein bar last till morning. And she had cash. Not much, but enough to get her by until she came up with a plan.

First she would call Conner to tell him what had happened. He would have to find a way home. With all that money in there, the sheriff's department would probably impound her car.

A whine sounded in the distance, gradually becoming louder and more shrill, shattering her already frayed nerves. Then the sirens stopped. The call to Conner would have to wait.

Reinforcements had arrived.

She pushed herself to her feet and ran like she had never run before.

EIGHT

Conner stepped around the dump truck he was working on and looked toward the office building in the distance. The sirens he'd heard were now silent, but they had sounded awfully close.

He immediately found their source. One Levy County Sheriff's vehicle was parked next to the building, two more at the back, lights flashing. Tension spread through him. Had some disgruntled former employee decided to take out his grievances on the others?

He removed his cell phone from his pocket and sent Darci a text—R U OK? When he tried to return to the truck that was demanding his attention, his focus was all over the place. He cast another glance at the building. If he drove up there, the deputies would probably shoo him away. But Darci was inside. It was all he could do to stand back and let law enforcement do its job.

But when ten minutes had passed with no

return text, he got into his truck and drove down the dirt road toward the office. He had to make sure that whatever had happened, it didn't involve Darci.

As he drew closer, though, activity in the parking lot told him it did. Two deputies stood at her car, the passenger door open. Wiggins was with them. Another deputy was headed toward the woods, a German shepherd leading the way. A fourth sheriff car pulled to a stop, and a deputy exited with another dog.

Conner's heart began to pound, and his palms grew clammy against the steering wheel. Had someone hurt Darci? Did it have anything to do with his tip about the bulldozer? If so, he would never forgive himself.

He pulled into an empty parking spot several spaces away and looked around. Where was Darci? Maybe she was holed up in her office, unaware of the excitement happening a few yards from the break room door.

Or maybe someone had attacked her, and she was unable to make it out of the building.

No, if anyone had been hurt, an ambulance would have arrived by now. The thought took the edge off the fear but didn't banish it. He wouldn't breathe easy until he saw her with his own eyes.

The deputy who had just arrived with the

dog approached Wiggins and the other two deputies. One handed him a black sweater, and he bent to let the dog sniff it.

A solid knot of worry formed in Conner's gut. The sweater looked just like one he'd seen Darci wear. Had someone kidnapped her? *Dear God, please protect her.* He frowned. Lately, he'd taken to praying quite a bit. But most of his prayers had been requests for help. He was too new at this whole God thing to know how He felt about that.

Conner got out of the truck and began walking toward the two men. He would volunteer to assist in any way possible. Maybe he could help organize a search party. The thought of Darci alone out there with a possible killer almost made him crazy.

He had nearly reached Darci's car when Wiggins turned and saw him. His eyes narrowed, but Conner kept his head high, his gait confident. Wiggins could bellow and bluster all he wanted. Darci was in danger, and he wasn't going to stand idly by.

One of the deputies addressed Wiggins. "Did anybody see the suspect leave?"

Conner hesitated, the sense that he'd misinterpreted something niggling at the back of his mind. Wiggins's next words confirmed it.

"No. She just walked out without saying anything to anybody."

Conner continued his path toward the break room door, relief warring with worry. No one had kidnapped her.

Darci wasn't the victim. She was the suspect.

As he reached for the doorknob, he kept his back to the other men. If Wiggins thought he had any interest in what happened to Darci, Conner would be unemployed before five o'clock.

He twisted the knob, ears straining to pick up Wiggins's words.

"I've suspected her of embezzling, so I've been watching her. I'm the one who called you guys. I think she knows I was onto her and was making plans to disappear. But when Deputy Bronson here showed up, it threw a monkey wrench in everything."

Conner swung open the door and stepped inside. Delaying any longer would rouse Wiggins's suspicions. He eased the door shut slowly, determined to gather every last bit of information he could. Wiggins was still talking.

"I'd love to know where that bag of money came from. My guess is Tucker's working with an accomplice. That cell phone might give you some leads."

Cell phone? A vise clamped down on his heart. Darci had run into the woods without her phone. In another three hours, she would be alone in the dark with no way to call out. And Wiggins and the police would have access to his and Darci's texts and a log of their phone calls. His days at P. T. were numbered.

He pulled the metal door shut, blocking out all sounds of the outside. His ringtone sounded, and he swiped left to reject the call. It had come from Darci's number. She had probably saved him as a contact, but he wasn't going to make it easy for Wiggins by answering.

After finishing his break, he returned to the field to complete work on the dump truck. Hopefully, it would run when he got it back together, because his mind was somewhere else. So was his heart.

What he really wanted to do was follow Darci into the woods and keep searching until he found her. But that was exactly what the deputies with the dogs were doing. If they didn't find her, his own chances were nil.

And he hoped with everything in him that they wouldn't find her. Jail was no place for someone as sweet and innocent as Darci.

But something seemed off about the whole situation. Why would Wiggins call in the law? Was he really confident that he'd covered all of his tracks so well that nothing would point to him?

Conner's ringtone sounded again, and he glanced at the screen. Another call from Darci's phone. Someone was awfully determined. He waited then played back his messages. A sweet female voice flowed through his phone, and his heart leaped. It was Darci. How was that possible? Wiggins had said she left her phone in her car.

He tensed as her words poured out.

"Conner, I'm in trouble." She sounded winded, as if she'd been running. Fear laced every word. "Wiggins has set me up. Please call me."

The second message was much the same as the first, except with a little more desperation. And he kicked himself for not taking each call when it came. Apparently, the phone left in her car wasn't hers.

When he redialed her, she picked up halfway through the first ring.

"Conner." The single word was heavy with relief.

"Where are you?"

"Splashing through a small creek, hoping and praying the dogs won't be able to pick up my scent."

"How can I find you?" He had to help her. He didn't know how, but he would find a way.

"You can't. You'd probably be followed. I don't even dare use my phone after this, because they'll be watching the activity. I've already called my mom and told her I won't be able to talk to her for the next few days." She sounded as if she was running. Quick gasps broke up her sentences. "But please call Hunter. Help him figure out a way to get me out of this."

His heart twisted. "I can't leave you alone out there."

"You have no choice. Hey, I'll be okay. I grew up camping with the children's group, then the teen group at church." She injected a touch of humor into her voice. "I'm great at roughing it."

Yep, that undying optimism. It came right through the phone. Except in Darci's case, it probably had more to do with faith than optimism. "You have food and water?"

"I've got a protein bar and a small bottle of water to get me through the night. And I have about forty dollars cash on me."

He still didn't like it. But she was right. He couldn't go to her. It would be too risky. He needed to come up with a plan.

"You can't live in the woods indefinitely.

Let me work on finding you a place to stay." He'd lived in Levy County all his life. Surely he could come up with someone who would be willing to put her up. "Can you get to a pay phone tomorrow or somewhere you can borrow a phone?"

"I'll have to find my way to civilization. I'm going to be really hungry come morning."

He released a relieved sigh. Tomorrow she would be around people. Of course, there was still tonight to get through—twelve or thirteen hours alone and unprotected in the darkness.

He tried to push the worry aside. He needed to focus. "I'm going to give you a friend's number. Call me on that at nine tomorrow." Hopefully, he could get ahold of Mike and he would be available then.

She stopped long enough to jot down the number, then resumed running, judging from the rustling and other noise coming through the phone.

He should probably get back to work before someone saw him goofing off on company time. But he didn't want to let her go. "How did you know to run? What tipped you off?"

"Wiggins fired me. I gathered up my stuff, and when I got out to my car, someone had left a present—a duffel bag full of cash and a cell phone. I was still trying to figure out what to do when Wiggins walked out with a Levy County Sheriff's deputy."

"He told the cops that you left without talking to anyone, that you'd probably figured out that he was onto you and made plans to disappear."

"That's a lie."

"Of course it's a lie. That's what Wiggins does best. But the cops don't have any reason not to believe him."

"I need you to find that reason, Conner."

"I'm going to try my best. Give me Hunter's number."

She did, then continued, "The rubber around my window was a little messed up, as if someone had used a Slim Jim to get in. But I can't prove it wasn't already like that."

"I'll give the information to Hunter. We'll get you out of this."

"Thank you."

There was a catch in her voice, and it tore him up. "Be careful."

"I will."

After hanging up, he placed a call to Mrs. Peggart. He was going to need a ride home. Then he would visit his friend Mike. Meanwhile, he needed to come up with a temporary home for Darci.

Throughout the afternoon, he mentally

crossed off one name after another. He knew lots of people, most of whom would be happy to do almost anything for him. But they would all draw the line at harboring a fugitive.

Except one—Nicki Jackson.

And that was the last person that he wanted to connect with Darci.

Nicki was a brief fling from his college days, and they had had infrequent contact since. The picture that she could paint of the twenty-year-old Conner Stevenson—wild, carefree and dating half the women on campus—was one he'd rather Darci not see.

But no matter how many other names crossed his mind, he kept coming back to Nicki. She was tough, but with a good heart. And she had just enough of a rebellious streak to have no qualms about going up against authority to see justice done. If she still lived in the same house as the last time he'd talked to her, she even had a small cottage out back that Darci could use. The setup was perfect.

He just couldn't shake the image of the two women sitting together into the wee hours of the morning, Nicki regaling Darci with every Conner Stevenson shenanigan she could remember.

It shouldn't matter so much. But it did, because he cared about what Darci thought of him. He admired and respected her. He enjoyed every minute he spent with her.

If he wasn't careful, he was going to find himself head over heels in love.

A truck turned off US 19 into the parking area next to Hershel's Quick Stop in Otter Creek. Its headlights cast the area in virtual daylight. Darci crept forward, remaining in the shadows. She wouldn't announce her presence until she'd identified the truck and driver beyond a doubt.

Last night, Conner had put together a plan and had filled her in on the details during their 9:00 a.m. phone conversation. She was to meet a woman with shoulder-length red hair who would be driving a silver Dodge Ram. If everything went as planned, she would sleep in a real bed tonight. After her ordeal of the past thirty-two hours, a hot shower and good night's sleep were worth a million bucks.

She'd kept her path in the creek until almost dusk, unwilling to risk getting out and leaving a scent the dogs could follow. Then she'd put her shoes back on and headed in what she'd hoped was the direction of the road. Once dusk gave way to night, she used the torch app on her phone to find her way. Fortunately, it had an almost full charge, because beyond the reaches of the beam, creatures moved through the darkness.

When she'd finally reached the road, she moved more quickly, but by the time she arrived in Otter Creek, it was almost 4:00 a.m. Taking a nap had been out of the question. Not only was she terrified that someone would sneak up on her, she also had to keep moving to stay warm.

The short-sleeved silk blouse and dress pants had been great attire for the office. So had the shoes with the two-inch wedge heels. But with temperatures dipping into the mid-fifties, she'd longed for her sweater several times. And the shoes had rubbed blisters on both feet before she had even reached the road.

Darci stopped to peer around the back corner of the building. The truck was gray or silver. And it was definitely a Dodge Ram. But she couldn't see into the darkened cab. She hesitated, trying to decide on a course of action. Then the driver's side window cranked down, and someone called her name in a hoarse whisper.

A breath she hadn't realized she'd been holding spilled out in a relieved sigh. She half ran, half limped from her hiding place and climbed up into the passenger seat. The driver held out her hand.

"I'm Nicki, Conner's friend from college. He told me about your situation. You can stay in the cottage. It's small, basically one room, but it's warm and comfortable."

"You can't imagine how wonderful that sounds." She let her head fall back against the seat.

According to Conner, Nicki could be trusted. But putting her life in the hands of a stranger set off all kinds of alarms. One simple phone call tipping off the police, and her life would be over.

But if she was going to survive, as well as stay out of jail, she was going to have to depend on someone other than herself.

Nicki backed out of the parking area, then headed south on US 19. Darci hadn't thought to ask Conner where Nicki lived. At this point, she didn't care. For the first time since yesterday afternoon, she was safe. She released a long sigh and let the tension drain away. Fatigue overtook her, and her eyes drifted shut.

"So how long have you and Conner been together?"

Nicki's question hung in the air for several seconds before penetrating the fog that engulfed Darci's brain.

"Together?" She lifted her head from the

seat. "Oh, it's not like that. We work together. That's all."

"Hearing Conner talk, I thought there was something more. But it doesn't surprise me. No one's been able to lasso his heart. Lots of women have tried. Conner just isn't one to be caged. About the time you think he's yours, you find out you've been personalizing what was nothing more than Stevenson charm."

Darci turned to look at her in the dim glow of the dashboard lights. Wistfulness seemed to have settled over her. Nicki wasn't just relating what she knew from observation. She was speaking from experience. She was an ex-girlfriend. Apparently one of many. And for some reason, that bothered Darci.

She shrugged it off. She was overly fatigued. That was all. How many women Conner dated—past, present and future—was no concern of hers.

But no matter how much she tried to tell herself that it didn't matter, the fact was, it did. She'd fallen victim to that Stevenson charm. And although there were all kinds of reasons not to, she was gradually falling in love with him.

She laid her head back against the seat and let her eyes close.

A hand on her shoulder some time later

startled her into wakefulness, and she looked around, unsure where she was.

"We're here."

Darci swiped the cobwebs from her brain, and it all came back to her. She was in Nicki's truck. Apparently she'd slept all the way to...

"Where are we?"

"Crystal River."

She put her purse over her shoulder and reached for the door handle. "Sorry. I didn't sleep last night."

"I figured as much."

Darci slid from the truck and looked around. Nicki lived in a rural area. There were no streetlights, no neighbors that she could see. On a dark night, it would be pitch-black, but tonight, a three-quarter moon bathed everything in its soft glow. Ahead of her was a small concrete blockhouse. Woods lay to the left, a pasture to the right.

"You're out in the boonies."

"I am. If you want to hide out and not be seen, this is the perfect place to do it."

Nicki led her past the house to an even smaller concrete block cottage, then unlocked and opened the door. When she flipped a switch, stark white light filled the tiny space.

Darci stepped inside and tilted her head downward. She'd now been in the same clothes for over forty hours. Mud stained the bottom of her pants. The knees and several places on her blouse were soiled from her fall. Over the tops of her shoes, her feet were filthy, and the wind had whipped her hair into a veritable bird's nest that would give the little travel brush she carried a major workout.

Nicki made a striking contrast in her scoop-necked T-shirt and designer jeans tucked into high-heeled boots. Her hair shone in the light, a shade of auburn that was much too bright to be natural. But it fit her well—bold, striking and beautiful.

So that was the kind of woman Conner dated. Nicki was unforgettable, one who would stand out in a crowd. Not only was she gorgeous, but her whole bearing exuded confidence. Actually, it was more than confidence. More like she knew her path and wasn't going to let anyone deter her from it.

But her smile was warm as she ushered Darci inside. She pointed to a closed door on the left.

"There are clean towels and washcloths on the counter in the bathroom. The TV works and is hooked up to cable, and the kitchen is furnished with all the eating utensils."

Darci followed Nicki through the one-room cottage. A living room occupied the front portion, with a couch, coffee table and TV. The kitchen in the rear left corner was just large enough for the needed appliances and bare minimum of cabinetry and held a two-person metal table. But most appealing of all was the daybed sitting in the right rear corner of the room.

Nicki opened a cabinet door. "I picked up some groceries. There's stuff in the fridge, too. Make a list, and I'll get anything else you need on my way home from work tomorrow."

"Thank you." Nicki had gone above and beyond. "Let me know what I owe you."

"Conner already took care of it."

"He met up with you?" Her heart began to pound. What had he been thinking? He could have been followed.

"No, he made an online transfer into my bank account. He's being super careful." She closed the cabinet door and leaned against the counter. "He bought a TracFone and has been using it to talk to me. He has one for you, too, but we've got to figure out how to get it here. Meanwhile, he'll talk to you on my phone."

Her pulse picked up and her stomach rolled over. She would still be able to talk to Conner during her confinement. Some of the heaviness lifted. Right now, he was her lifeline.

Nicki moved toward the small chest of drawers next to the bed. "I'm also leaving you some of my yoga pants and T-shirts, along with a few sweat suits. I'm a little taller than you, but they should fit."

"I can't thank you enough for all this."

Nicki waved away her gratitude. "It's no big deal. The place is sitting empty anyway. I used to rent it out, but a couple of deadbeat tenants cured me of that. Now I just let friends crash here when they visit."

Nicki moved toward the front of the cottage. "I'm going to let you get some rest now. If you need anything, just knock on my back door."

Darci twisted the lock behind her, then crossed the room to pull a T-shirt and pair of stretchy pants from the drawer. *Thank You, Lord.* If it weren't for Conner and Nicki, she'd be spending another night in the woods, struggling to stay warm and hiding from predators—two-legged and four-legged. Instead, she had food and shelter and company, even if that company came in the form of Conner's beautiful ex.

After a relaxing hot shower, she slipped into clean clothes, pulled back the bedspread and slid between the sheets. She would probably be out cold within moments. If only the nightmares would stay at bay.

As she pulled the covers to her chin, she prayed for a night filled with sweet dreams.

Dreams of Conner.

NINE

Tracks crisscrossed in the sand, an intricate pattern of ridges and valleys left behind by massive tires. Now, a few minutes before the start of the workday, all the equipment was silent. And Conner stalked the area, eyes peeled for Captain America.

Knowing that Kyle was nuts over any and all things Avengers, Jerry, the scale operator, had given Conner the action figure yesterday at lunchtime, and he'd put it in his pocket. But when he got home, it was gone. It had to have fallen out when he removed his keys. But he'd just finished combing the entire area, and the figure had vanished. He would have to declare Captain America missing in action.

Conner headed toward the fenced equipment area to pick up the service truck, and his eyes fell on a small patch of blue at the deepest part of one of the tracks. He bent to brush aside the sand and unearthed a crushed Captain America.

His brows creased in confusion. Yesterday, he'd left at the same time as everyone else. And none of the operators had started yet this morning.

Which meant one thing. Someone had used the backhoe last night after the mine had closed.

At ten o'clock, Conner headed for the scale house. He would spend his morning break with Jerry. After chatting a few minutes, he pulled the action figure from his pocket.

Jerry's brows shot up. "Whoa, what happened to it?"

"It fell out of my pocket when I got my keys out yesterday. I didn't realize it till I got home."

"Someone did a number on it this morning."

"Not this morning. Last night. I found this buried in a track before the guys had cranked up a single piece of equipment. The tracks match the tires on the Caterpillar backhoe."

Jerry shook his head. "That doesn't make sense. P. T. doesn't run a night shift. Once we head out of here at five o'clock, the day is done."

"That's what I thought. But this proves otherwise. I'm afraid someone might be tampering with the equipment."

"That's not good. Have you told Wiggins?"

Conner searched his eyes. Of all the P. T. employees, Jerry was the one he'd gotten closest to. But could he trust him? He didn't have access to the information he needed to prove Darci's innocence, so he was going to have to trust someone. He'd rather it be Jerry than anyone else.

"I'm afraid Wiggins might be involved. What do you know about him?"

"Other than that he's an arrogant jerk?" Jerry smiled. "Frankly, I don't have a whole lot of love for the man. We keep hoping Peter Turlong will come back and clean house."

"Wiggins isn't my favorite person, either, especially after what he's done to Darci."

Jerry nodded slowly. "When I heard that she'd been caught embezzling funds then fled the police, I knew there was more to the story. That doesn't sound like the Darci Tucker I know."

No, it didn't sound like the Darci Tucker he knew, either. But things weren't looking good. He'd talked to Hunter several times over the past three and a half days. Although no official charges had been filed, she was wanted for questioning. They believed that, whatever she was involved in, she was working with an accomplice who'd dropped his phone when delivering the money. Several calls between that phone and Darci's confirmed their suspicions. The number was the same one she'd asked Hunter to check.

Determination entered Jerry's eyes. "What can I do to help?"

"The signs coming onto the property say it's under video surveillance. Is that true?"

"Yeah, parts of it, anyway. Several years ago, we had some theft—one of the carts that the managers ride around on and a bunch of mechanics' tools. Turlong had the cameras installed then. And just in case that wasn't going to be enough, he got Genghis for backup."

Yeah, Genghis. Conner had met the pit bull that guarded the fenced equipment area his first day there. Since the two of them had been formally introduced, the dog would supposedly not bother him. But he always breathed a sigh of relief once someone had gotten him securely chained up.

"Is it possible to get our hands on the tape from last night?"

"I don't know about the actual tape, but I believe the activity is still being backed up on the cloud."

That was even better. "How can I view that?"

"You'll need the URL and password. Let me see what I can do."

"Try not to arouse any suspicion, okay?"

"Hey, if I just say we're trying to bring Wiggins down, we'll have the cooperation of everyone here. But no, I'll be discreet."

By lunchtime, Jerry had the requested information, and by the end of the day, Conner had formulated a plan to safely view the footage. There would even be a side benefit. He would get to see Darci.

He pulled from the gravel drive onto the asphalt and headed for home. It had been four days since Darci had taken off. Ever since, no matter where he went, someone seemed to be following. Whether law enforcement or Wiggins's people, they were keeping him on a tight leash.

He eased off the gas to make the final turn onto 92nd Place. The Crown Victoria that had followed him until that point continued on. But he wasn't fooled. It, or another one like it, would be at the ready, should he decide to leave the house.

When he stopped next to the yellow Volkswagen Bug, he pulled the TracFone from his pocket and brought up Nicki's number. Mrs. Peggart would have things well under control inside. She'd whipped Kyle into shape in no time and had done it in a way that Kyle had hardly noticed. If only he could make her child-rearing techniques work for him.

But it didn't really matter. His mom had assured him that they would be ready to take Kyle back by Christmas. That was only a week away. Oddly enough, the thought no longer brought the sense of relief that it had before, the feeling that he'd just crawled out from under a two-ton weight. Instead, it left him with a hollowness in his gut and a hole in his heart. He was getting attached to the kid.

Conner touched the screen and put the phone to his ear. When Nicki answered, he didn't waste time with pleasantries.

"I'm going to see you guys tonight." Viewing the security footage on his own computer was a bad idea. He was being watched too closely, had possibly already been hacked. But Nicki...

"Are you nuts?" Her voice raised in both pitch and volume on the last word. "You need to stay put. I don't want you bringing anybody down on us—good guys *or* bad guys."

"Don't worry. Everything's okay. I have a plan."

Two hours later, Conner pulled into the Walmart Supercenter parking lot in Chiefland. After calling Nicki, he had made a quick trip to the library to try out the URL and password Jerry had provided. They had worked, and there was no log of online views. Mike had come right after dinner to pick up Kyle and would keep him all night, if necessary.

And he'd taken a few minutes for a call to Hunter. Darci's cop friend had nothing further to report. They would keep feeding each other whatever information they had—except Darci's whereabouts. Hunter had cautioned him the night Darci fled. If he knew where she was, he couldn't keep it a secret without risking the loss of his badge.

As usual, a dark-colored SUV had been behind him from the time he pulled off his street until he turned into Walmart. It was probably at that moment circling the parking lot, its driver watching for him to return to his truck. Someone was going to be watching for a long time.

He stepped through the automatic door and took a shopping cart. He'd parked near the grocery section, but that wasn't where he would exit. As he strolled through the aisles, gradually filling his cart, guilt pricked him. He was going to abandon everything. At least he would avoid the refrigerator and freezer areas.

He finished in the food section, then made his way across the store, occasionally adding an item to the cart. His last stop was the garden center. Three customers milled around, and a clerk stood near the cash register, arranging plants on the clearance display. Conner checked his phone for the time. In another five minutes, a text would arrive.

It came through two minutes early. He parked his cart at the end of the patio pavers and made his way toward the open gate. The clerk glanced at him, and he nodded. Just as he stepped outside, a silver Ram stopped in front of him. He climbed inside and pulled the door shut. The truck began to move immediately. But he was already leaning far to the left, his face near the seat. To anyone looking in, it would appear Nicki was alone.

After she'd driven for a minute, Conner lifted his head. "Does anyone seem to be following?"

A firm hand pushed him back down. "Not yet, but stay low."

Nicki didn't give him the go-ahead until they had traveled some distance on Highway 19-98. He rubbed his stiff back and neck, then lifted his hand for a high five. "We did it. We outsmarted them."

"Don't count your chickens before they hatch. I've still got to get you back."

"That'll be the easy part. I'll have you drop

me off several blocks away and disappear. Then I'll walk back to Walmart and get my truck."

Right now, nothing would dampen his enthusiasm. After four days of only telephone contact, he was finally going to see Darci. The way his heart was racing, he was as bad as a teenager experiencing his first crush. He needed to get a grip.

He'd fought his attraction toward her, not allowing their relationship to progress beyond friendship. But this separation was making him crazy. It was also forcing him to admit that he was falling for her. Hard.

Unfortunately, he couldn't act on it. If he did, parting would be that much harder when the time came. And eventually it would. Darci would go back to her life with Jayden, and his mother would take Kyle. And he would once again be free and single.

And lonely and bored.

But that was no reason to involve Darci in his general dissatisfaction with life.

Nicki glanced over at him in the darkness. "You're awfully quiet."

"I have a lot on my mind."

A long moment passed before she spoke again. "I told Darci that no woman has ever been able to lasso your heart."

Great. Just what he'd feared. He'd been the topic of at least one conversation.

"I was wrong." Her voice was low, her tone heavy with meaning.

She drew to a stop in her driveway, then led him down a sidewalk to the cottage in the back—Darci's temporary home. Nicki raised her hand to knock, and the door swung open before her fist could make contact.

Darci stood there in a pale blue T-shirt and black yoga pants—loaners, no doubt—her hair brushed to a fine sheen and falling freely over her shoulders. And all his good intentions fell away like icicles thawing over a roaring fire.

A flood of emotion swept through him, overwhelming in its power. Without a word, he wrapped her in a hug and crushed her to him. Her arms went around his waist, the strength of her own grip rivaling his.

His mouth sought hers, and when their lips met, a jolt shot all the way to his toes. A little voice in the back of his mind tried to tell him that what he was doing was wrong, that he should pull away and apologize. But never had anything felt so right, especially with the way she was kissing him back, without reservation.

Nicki cleared her throat, shattering the moment.

"Coworkers, are we?"

* * *

Darci pulled away and brought her hand to her lips as heat crept up her cheeks. She'd told Nicki that she and Conner weren't a couple, that they only worked together.

Conner had just made a liar out of her. And she'd done nothing to dissuade him. In fact, she'd encouraged him. It was the first time in five years that anyone had been able to slip past the defenses she'd erected around her heart.

Her gaze locked with his. None of the confusion and embarrassment swirling inside her was reflected in his eyes. Instead there was conviction.

"That's something we might havc to reassess." He took both of her hands in his. "I've been so worried about you. Are you okay?"

She nodded, swallowing hard. How was she supposed to carry on an intelligent conversation after his kiss had fried all her brain circuits?

"I got a new lead today."

"What kind of lead?"

"Something going on at the mine. I'm not sure yet what it is, but we're going to use Nicki's computer to see what we can find out."

She pulled away from him, panic building

inside her. "We can't. Wiggins will know and he'll find me."

He once again grasped her hands. "No, this is different. We're going to look at the surveillance footage at the mine. Everything is backed up to the cloud. Jerry gave me the URL and password today."

"What if there's a log kept?"

"There isn't. I already checked."

"Come on." Nicki still stood at the door. "I'll take you two over there."

As Darci followed, uneasiness descended on her with every step. There were too many times over the past few weeks when she'd done something, only to find out later she was being watched. But Conner had already checked it out. And he was careful.

Nicki unlocked her back door and ushered them inside. This was where Darci had been spending her evenings. After being cooped up in the cottage all day while Nicki worked, getting out for a few hours helped her maintain her sanity. She'd even cooked the past two nights so they could share dinner.

They had plenty to talk about, whether discussing Conner or not, although he had been a favorite topic. Nicki had known him a long time and had a large repertoire of stories. And she'd confirmed what Darci had already suspected—Conner wasn't a settling-down kind of guy. Regardless of how much emotion had gone into that kiss.

Once they were seated on the couch, Nicki handed Conner her laptop. He removed a slip of paper from his shirt pocket and typed in the URL and password recorded there.

"We can view it live while it's happening, or we can go back and look at previously recorded footage." He made a couple of clicks. "I dropped something before getting into my truck yesterday afternoon. When I came in this morning, it had been run over by the backhoe. Something went on there last night, and I'd like to find out what." He clicked the mouse two more times. "This is the camera that covers that area, and this footage is from Monday night, starting at 8:00." He clicked again. "I'm putting it on fast forward, so we don't have to stare at mounds of sand for eight or ten hours."

Even on fast-forward, the surveillance was uneventful. Fortunately, the conversation over the next hour was a bit more entertaining. Nicki was well into a story about an elaborate hoax that she and her girlfriends had played on some guys in college when Darci's breath hitched. Something had moved across the screen, or partway across the screen.

She held up a hand. "Wait. Rewind that."

Conner did as she asked, then played it back, this time on regular speed. A couple of minutes passed before the recording reached that point again.

He nodded. "It's an owl."

"Something's wrong." Darci shook her head. "Play it again." When he did, she pointed at a place two-thirds of the way across the screen. "The owl disappears right here. If the camera picked it up, it seems as if the path should have gone all the way across. Instead, that bird disappears into thin air."

Nicki leaned forward to look at her past Conner. "What do you think it means?"

She shook her head. "I don't know. Maybe somebody stopped the recording."

Conner let it continue to play. "No, it's still going. See the time display?"

"Go back to fast-forward. Let's see if anything else looks strange."

A few minutes later, Conner tensed next to her, then clicked to pause and rewind. Nicki leaned closer as an object started across the screen. "It's another bird."

As before, it disappeared two thirds of the way across.

"Or the same one." Conner stopped the video again. "Did anyone pay any attention to the time on the other one?"

Darci struggled to recall the numbers. "When you said the time was still going, it was 9:53. So a minute or two before that, I'd say."

"And now it's 10:21." Conner jotted down the two times. "Thirty minutes apart."

He restarted the video, and the bird appeared again at 10:51. The rest of the night was uneventful. He closed the computer. "I'd say that what we're seeing from 10:51 on is the real thing."

Darci agreed. "But starting at 9:51, the recording was set on two loops."

Conner shook his head. "Someone really knows this equipment. I couldn't begin to explain how they altered the recording, then uploaded it to the cloud. The sad part of it is they would have gotten away with it if it weren't for the owl deciding to fly across the path of the camera at that exact moment."

Darci frowned. "So we know that something happened at the mine last night between 9:51 and 10:51."

Conner nodded. "Something that someone has gone to a whole lot of trouble to keep secret."

TEN

"I think you need to give it a try."

Darci turned toward Nicki and cocked a brow. "Give what a try?"

"A relationship with Conner. I can tell you're thinking about him."

Yeah. Thinking about Conner had become a favorite pastime, second only to *being* with Conner.

She propped her feet on the coffee table next to the popcorn bowl, empty now except for a few kernels. She and Nicki had just finished watching a movie, a romantic comedy. Probably not the best choice in her state of mind.

Conner's kiss last night had left her more confused than ever. They didn't have that kind of relationship.

She sighed. "No one can lasso Conner's heart. You said it yourself."

"I made that statement before I saw him with you. That boy's got it bad."

Darci frowned. "I think you've got an overactive imagination."

There was definitely attraction. It had been there right from the start, at least on her end. And unless she had misinterpreted the warmth in his eyes, she'd sparked his interest fairly early, too.

But moving from attraction to the kind of kiss they'd shared last night was a huge step, one she wasn't ready to take. And based on everything she knew about Conner, he wasn't, either. He probably never would be.

Nicki crossed her arms. "You're living in denial. I've known Conner for a long time, and I've never seen him like this. He can't keep his eyes off you."

"It'll pass. Like you said, just when you think he's crazy about you, you find out it's nothing more than that Stevenson charm."

Nicki glared at her, but there was humor behind it. "You're going to make me eat my words, aren't you? What I saw last night went way beyond Stevenson charm."

Heat crept into her cheeks at the reminder. "It doesn't matter. It's not a choice I'm at liberty to make. I have a child to think about."

"So? Children always do better in two-parent homes. They've done studies on that."

What Nicki said was true. But there were factors she didn't know about.

"Jayden isn't your typical child. He's got autism. There's a chance that he might be with me for the rest of my life. He's *my* responsibility, not Conner's or anyone else's."

"But if Conner is willing to assume that responsibility, it benefits both you and Jayden."

Darci shook her head. Nicki made it sound so simple. It was anything but.

Right now, a common cause had thrown them together. Conner needed to bust Wiggins to get justice for his sister. She needed to bust Wiggins to clear herself. Once that was accomplished, would there be enough to keep them together? Probably not.

She glanced at the clock, then rose from the couch. It was a few minutes after ten, and though Nicki usually had Saturdays off, tomorrow morning she would have to work. "I'll think about it. Okay?"

"That's all I ask."

As Darci made her way along the stepping stones, Nicki watched from her back door. Before closing her own, Darci waved good-night to her new friend.

Gratitude welled up inside her. She was in the valley now, deeper than any she'd ever experienced. But God was with her. And He had provided encouragement and support in the form of Conner and Nicki.

She locked the door, then pulled a phone from her pocket and laid it on the coffee table. It wasn't her android. If anyone checked that account, the last call would be the one from Conner Monday afternoon. What she had now was the TracFone he'd given her last night.

She changed into the pants and T-shirt she'd selected as her nightwear and eyed the stack of books on the coffee table. Boredom had been driving her crazy, so at her request, Nicki had stopped at the library after work today and chosen books from a variety of genres. Christmas had arrived early.

Darci eased onto the couch and reached for the stack. There were two historicals, a time travel, a contemporary romance, a women's fiction and a fantasy. Two genres were missing—suspense and horror. Nicki apparently figured she didn't need anything to scare her or keep her on the edge of her seat. She had enough of that in real life.

After reading the blurbs on each, she settled on the time travel. Partway into the second chapter, her new phone rang. She smiled. Since Conner and Nicki were the only ones who had the number, it was probably Conner.

Instead, it was Nicki's number that showed

up on the display. She swiped the screen and pressed the phone to her ear.

"Run!" The single word was shrill and laced with panic.

She shot to her feet at the same time the door exploded inward. Two men stormed in, both in ski masks. Her heart pounded against her rib cage, sending blood roaring through her ears, and she lunged for the back door. With shaking fingers, she twisted the top lock. One more to go.

A hand tightened on her shoulder and spun her around. The next moment, a gloved fist connected with the left side of her jaw, snapping her head sideways and sending pain shooting through the side of her face. The phone clattered to the floor.

She backed away, hands outstretched, until the side of the kitchen cabinets stopped her. The beast of a man towered over her, reeking of cigarette smoke. He took a step closer, and she twisted and ducked, then ran for the front door.

But the other man stood guard in the damaged opening like an evil sentry, his arms crossed over his chest. He was smaller than the man who had hit her, but it might as well have been a squad of soldiers blocking the door.

She skidded to a stop and spun around. The

beast moved closer, clenching his fists. Her gaze shot to the back door. If she could make it around him and out, she could probably outrun him. It was her only hope. *God, help me.*

But as she sprinted past him, he grabbed her shirt, bringing her to an abrupt halt. Blue eyes locked with hers, startling in their intensity. But the coldness in their depths chilled her to the core. He was going to hit her again.

No. She couldn't handle another blow. A scream welled up in her throat but was cut short as pain exploded across her mind. Tiny points of light danced in front of her, and shadows darkened the edges of her vision. Her knees buckled, and he released her shirt, letting her fall forward.

But he wasn't finished with her. He grabbed a fistful of her hair and pulled until she was upright, resting on her knees. Blood had pooled in her mouth, and her tongue had become thick and stiff.

Then he continued his assault, slamming a boot into her right side. A cry came up her throat, half guttural moan and half scream. He released her hair, and she fell sideways, the blood that had pooled in her mouth running out onto the tile floor.

She drew up her knees and curled into a fetal position. Her ribs screamed in agony with each jagged breath. There was no one to help her. The blessing of no close neighbors to meddle in her business was turning out to be a curse. *Dear God, please just let it end.*

Her tormentor slowly circled her, then stopped in front of her. He shifted his weight to one foot, and she squeezed her eyes shut, bracing herself for the next blow.

"Hey, take it easy." The voice came from the direction of the front door. "He wants her scared, not dead."

Footsteps sounded against the tile floor, and she lifted one eyelid. The man stepped to the side and retrieved her phone from the floor. For a half minute, he stood with his back to her. Then he laid the phone on the coffee table and followed the other man outside.

A heavy silence fell over the house, and she lay motionless, body screaming in pain. Finally, she pushed herself upright and clutched her side. She likely had some cracked ribs. And though she wanted nothing more than to lie down and sleep, she needed to check on Nicki and call Conner.

She slowly got to her feet, wincing with each movement. The door had been ripped from its hinges, the jamb splintered. Lead settled in her gut. She had not only put Nicki in danger, she'd also gotten her property damaged. First thing tomorrow morning, she would leave. She had no idea where she would go, but she couldn't stay here any longer.

When she stepped outside, Nicki was halfway up the walk, still dressed in the clothes she'd been in earlier. Darci watched her close the remaining distance, then gasped when she moved into the light. Her lower lip was puffy, and blood had dried at the corner of her mouth. One eye had swollen partially shut.

Darci swallowed hard, guilt stabbing her. She should never have come here. "Are you okay?"

"More okay than you are. You'd better see a doctor."

"I can't. You know my story."

Nicki nodded. "The police are on the way. I'm sorry. I couldn't let those guys kill you."

The kindness in Nicki's eyes almost broke her, and she had to fight back tears. "I understand. What did you tell them?"

"I didn't say anything about you. I said that two guys busted my door down and started to beat me up but left when I screamed. All that was true. I just left out some details." She gave her a half smile, then winced. "I'm sure they'll check things out back here. Get your stuff together, and I'll clean up the blood. Take some food with you. There are plastic bags under the sink."

A faint squeal sounded in the distance. Darci pushed the pain to the back of her mind and limped into the kitchen. By the time she'd filled the first bag, Nicki had finished her task and grabbed another empty bag.

The sirens moved closer. Nicki opened a dresser drawer and removed some items.

Darci protested, "Those are yours."

"Take them."

A minute later, she moved to the back door with two grocery bags over one arm and a third bag and her purse over the other. Her new phone was inside.

"Wait." Nicki stepped on the heel of one tennis shoe and pulled her foot out. After doing the same with the other, she stripped off both socks. "Those sandals I picked up for you aren't going to do it."

Darci's eyes stung as tears threatened. "How can I ever repay you?"

Nicki pressed the tennis shoes and socks into her arms. "Just stay alive."

The sirens increased in volume, their shrillness rending the quiet night. Then they fell silent. The police were right out front.

Nicki ran to meet them, and Darci slipped out the back. The darkness wrapped around her, and she felt more alone than she had since the whole ordeal began. It was getting harder and harder to trust God and hang on to her optimism. No, not optimism. Faith.

Since coming back to God at the end of her senior year of college, never once had her faith faltered. Not through Jayden's diagnosis and not through the struggles she faced raising a special-needs child alone. Now she was having her faith tested daily. Hourly.

She squared her shoulders and raised her chin. She would keep reminding herself that, no matter what happened, God was in control. He was always in control.

The TracFone rang, and a number she didn't recognize displayed on the screen. She put it to her ear with a tentative "Hello."

"Hello, Tucker." It was Wiggins. She would recognize that condescending tone anywhere. "Did you enjoy your little visit?"

Anger coursed through her. The moment the men burst into the cottage, she was sure Wiggins had sent them. But hearing him gloat almost sent her over the edge.

She drew in a stabilizing breath. "What do you want?"

"Your confession. Turn yourself in and admit to embezzling, and I'll see to it that all the charges are dropped. Then disappear. Let your little investigation go, and never set foot on P. T. property again."

"Forget it."

"Listen, Tucker. If you try to go up against me, you're making a big mistake."

"No, Wiggins. *You're* the one making a big mistake. You're underestimating me."

She lowered the phone and ended the call. Wiggins had said he would get the charges dropped. He was making empty promises. He didn't have that authority.

According to what Conner had learned from Hunter, she hadn't been officially charged. She was just wanted for questioning. But those charges were coming. Once the authorities sifted through all the information, she would have a lot more to fight than attempting to elude a law enforcement officer.

Unless Wiggins had no plans to provide the evidence to charge her with. It would make sense. If he gave the police what they would need to put her away, he risked getting himself arrested.

His plan to keep her quiet by framing her had backfired. So maybe this was plan B. But if plan B involved her confessing to a crime she didn't commit, it wasn't going to work out for him any better than plan A had.

When her phone rang again, she glanced at

the screen, then let it go to voice mail. There was nothing Wiggins had to say that she needed to hear.

A few minutes later, she pulled her phone out again. If Wiggins was brash enough to record a threat, it could work to her advantage. The single message began to play.

"Hanging up on me wasn't wise, Tucker." Although there was the hint of something familiar, the airy tone and feigned Italian accent disguised his voice well. "I know where your parents live. You do as I say, or not only will *you* disappear, but that little boy of yours will, too."

Darci lowered the phone, her blood turning to ice in her veins.

Wiggins had threatened her so many times, it was starting to lose its effect.

But now he was threatening her son.

And that changed everything.

Conner picked up his phone and checked the time. Darci was spending the evening with Nicki, as usual, but at well after ten, she should be back at the cottage. Now that he'd gotten her own phone to her, he could call her whenever he wanted without bothering Nicki.

Before he could pull up her number, the phone rang in his hand. He put it to his ear.

"Hi, sweetheart. I was just getting ready to call you, but you beat me to it."

"I had to leave Nicki's."

The bluntness of her words, as well as the desperation behind them, instantly squashed his enthusiasm. "Why? What happened?"

"Wiggins found me and sent a couple of goons to punch a little fear into me."

Fire shot through him at the thought of anyone hurting her. If he could get his hands on Wiggins at that moment, Wiggins would be on his way to the hospital and he would be on his way to jail.

The realization that followed was a sucker punch to the gut. It was his fault. He'd led them to her. No one had been following when he and Nicki left Walmart. But Wiggins had men watching for his return. And even though Nicki had dropped him off a few blocks away, someone had seen them, then followed her home.

"This is my fault. I'm so sorry."

"Don't blame yourself. You took all kinds of precautions."

But he *did* blame himself. He'd been acting on his own selfish desires. He'd wanted to see her, so he'd found a way.

But beating himself up was accomplishing nothing. "Did you recognize either of the men?"

"No, they had ski masks on. The man at the door was the right height and build to be Jimmy Fuller. But I can't imagine him standing by and watching the beating that I took. Of course, if he's involved with Wiggins, he'd probably do anything to keep from getting caught."

Conner ground his teeth. Another reason to dislike Fuller. "How about the other one?"

"He was big, probably six foot, and he had blue eyes, a vivid aqua blue. If I ever see him again, I'd recognize them instantly."

"Did they talk to you at all?"

"The big guy didn't say a word. But after he'd beat me half senseless, the other guy told him to take it easy."

The longing to be with her was so overwhelming it hurt. "Where are you?"

"Hiding out in the woods near Nicki's house. She sent food with me, a couple of changes of clothes and a light jacket, all hers. She even gave me the shoes off her feet."

"They fit you?"

"They're a couple sizes too big, but I'm managing. I owe her a lot. I don't know what I would have done the last few days without her."

Gratitude underscored her words, in spite of

her bleak circumstances. That thankful spirit was something he loved about her.

She lowered her voice. "Wiggins threatened Jayden."

"You talked to Wiggins?"

"The guy who hit me picked up my phone before he left and called Wiggins so he'd have my number. When Wiggins called, he told me to turn myself in and admit to embezzling, and he would have the charges dropped."

"You don't believe him, do you?"

"Not for a second. When I wouldn't agree to his demands, he threatened Jayden. I called my mom, and they'll be on their way to North Carolina with him shortly. They have a place outside of Murphy."

Worry slithered through him. If Wiggins's people saw Nicki drop him off in the wee hours of the morning, Darci's parents would never make it off Cedar Key. "Did you warn them to make sure they're not being followed?"

"Yes. I told them to call Hunter."

"So what do we do now? You need a safe place to stay."

"I'm going to find out what Wiggins is doing."

His chest tightened, and though he didn't want to hear the answer, he asked the question anyway. "How do you intend to do that?"

"I'm going to camp out in the woods at the mine and stay there until I get to the bottom of it. Claire saw something, something she was convinced would put Wiggins away."

"And it got her killed."

"What choice do I have?" Desperation filled her tone.

"Let the police handle it."

"And what do we tell them? We think there's something shady going on but have no idea what?" The desperation had given way to sarcasm. "We don't have any evidence to take to the police."

She was right. They couldn't ask the authorities to investigate based on a hunch.

"I'm not letting you do this alone."

"You're being watched. I think we found that out tonight."

He cringed at the reminder. "Give me some time. I'll figure out a way."

As soon as he ended the call, he began to pace. Kyle was asleep, having gone to bed a long time ago. The TV was on low, a movie that he'd lost interest in shortly after it had started. He walked into the kitchen to get a drink of water, then returned to the living room. And an idea began to form.

He picked up his phone. It was late, too late

to be making calls. Mike would just have to forgive him. So would Mrs. Peggart.

He finished the two brief conversations, then pocketed his phone with a smile.

He had a plan.

Conner stepped out of the woods that bordered the rear of Mike's house, a pack strapped to his back and two motorcycle helmets in his hands. His friend had been holding on to his bike for the past week, more than enough time for the promised tune-up. Tonight Conner needed it back.

Instead of circling around to the front of the house, he knocked on the back door. Fortunately, Mike lived only a mile away, because he'd made the entire trip on foot, slipping out his own back door as soon as darkness had fallen and staying under the cover of trees as much as possible.

Mike stepped out onto the patio. "As promised, it's all ready." He led him toward a large carport that held an old Mustang, a four-wheeler and two bikes. The Suzuki was Conner's.

Mike eyed the backpack and handed him the key. "I'm not even going to ask what you're up to."

"Good, because I wouldn't tell you." He

pulled a couple of bills out of his wallet. After strapping one helmet to the back, he put on his own and settled himself onto the seat.

Within a few minutes, he was on Highway 19-98 headed south, ticking off the miles between Chiefland and Crystal River. Mrs. Peggart had agreed to spend the night. So he could focus his entire attention on Darci.

He turned from 19 onto Turkey Oak, then slowed as he approached 495, scanning the edges of the road. This was where they were to meet. But after he pulled off, a half minute passed with no sign of her. Then she stepped out of the woods carrying her purse and some plastic bags. When she crossed into the beam of his headlight, his heart dropped to his knees and almost stopped.

A fist-size bruise covered the left side of her jaw, and that side of her lower lip had ballooned to twice its normal size. Her right cheek was a matching shade of purple, with swelling that extended into her eyelid, pulling it halfway closed.

He threw the kickstand down and rushed to her, drawing her into his arms.

She immediately stiffened. "Don't squeeze. I think I have some cracked ribs."

"Wiggins is going to pay for this." The words bore the strength of a promise.

For several moments, he held her, emotions at war within him—fury at Wiggins for everything he'd put her through, determination to see justice done and tenderness toward the woman in his arms, so sweet and gentle and caring.

And he had to name one more: love. He couldn't deny it any longer. Though he'd fought it with everything in him, he'd fallen in love with Darci Tucker.

But regardless of what he felt for her, he wouldn't pursue anything permanent. Because if he did, he would fail miserably. Just like his dad and the string of stepdads that followed. He couldn't do that to Darci.

He reluctantly released her, took the bags from her and handed her the other helmet. After he secured her bags and shifted the pack to his front, she settled in behind him and wrapped her arms around his waist. A half mile from the mine, he pulled off the road and killed the engine.

"We'll push this into the woods so it's hidden from the road. Then we'll hike in. Are you up to it?"

"You'd better believe it."

He again strapped the pack to his back and gripped the handlebars of the bike. The night was quiet, the silence broken only by the crunch of the leaves and pine needles beneath their feet. Traffic on the road behind them was nonexistent.

"I think this is good."

He removed a small flashlight from his pocket, then took her hand. They would stay just inside the woods along the road, then move in deeper along the gravel drive leading into the mine. He wouldn't risk the cameras picking up their movements.

"So what's inside the pack?"

"Snacks, a couple of bottles of water, a thin blanket and a video camera. Have you eaten today?"

"Yes, dry cereal for breakfast, a can of soup for lunch and a can of beans and hot dogs for dinner. All cold, of course. But I'm just thankful that Nicki had stocked the kitchen with lots of cans that had pop tops."

"What about water?"

"I have two water bottles that I've kept filled from public water fountains."

"Good." Darci was resourceful. And she was smart. If anyone could take care of herself, she could.

He stopped walking and removed the pack from his back. "This is the closest we can get to where I saw the backhoe tracks and still be hidden."

After pulling the blanket from the pack, he spread it out on the ground. Then they settled down to wait. Hopefully, something would happen soon.

Or it was going to be a long night.

ELEVEN

"Darci, wake up."

The words seemed to come from a distance, hollow and faint, and she tried to tune them out. She was comfortable and content and wasn't going to let anything intrude.

"Sweetheart."

She turned away from the sound. Then a hand on her shoulder brought her instantly awake. She bolted upright with a gasp.

"Sorry I startled you." Conner was on one knee, looking down at her, bathed in filtered moonlight.

She shook her head to clear it. "I fell asleep." She was in the woods, exposed and vulnerable. But she'd felt secure enough in Conner's presence to actually sleep.

"It's eleven o'clock, and someone's coming up the drive."

Now that Conner mentioned it, she heard it, too, the crunch of gravel and the hum of an engine. He extended a hand and pulled her to her feet. A half minute later, a pickup truck appeared around the corner of the office building and continued its path away from them. It came to a stop near the Caterpillar backhoe. A moment later, a man stepped out.

Conner leaned toward her. "Do you know him?"

Darci squinted into the darkness. A half-moon shone from a cloudless sky, but it didn't offer enough light for her to identify the man at that distance. "I can't tell."

The backhoe cranked up and a spotlight on top came on. Then it turned and started to crawl toward them. Less than a hundred feet from where they stood, it stopped and began to dig. Its claw-lined bucket plunged into the earth again and again, creating a mountain of dirt next to an ever-widening hole. Someone was getting ready to bury something—something big, based on the size of the hole.

She looked past him to the mounds in the distance. The mine extended for several hundred acres behind and to the right of the offices. But none of the mining work happened this close to the woods. Tonight's activities weren't related to the operations of P. T. Aggregates.

Finally the man stopped digging and shut

off the backhoe. The spot stayed on. The door on the side opened, and he stepped down and lit a cigarette.

"Now do you recognize him?" Conner's voice was a soft whisper. With the backhoe off, everything was once again wrapped in silence.

"Not at all." He wasn't an employee of P. T. He was a big guy with an air of toughness. As he stood with his feet planted wide, taking long drags on his cigarette, she hoped neither of them would have to tangle with him.

But maybe she already had. He was the right size to be the guy who had beat her up. And he was a smoker. Chances were good that if she got close enough to see his eyes, they would be a deep, vivid blue.

When another vehicle made its way up the drive, the backhoe operator flicked his cigarette onto the sand and ground it out with the sole of his shoe. He waited with his arms crossed as a car rounded the back corner of the building. Wiggins's Mercedes.

Conner unzipped the pack, removed his video camera and set it to record. Wiggins pulled into a parking space, then got out and approached the other man. Conner followed his movement with the camera.

"They'll be here in thirty minutes." Wiggins's words were terse. "You done?"

"I'm ready."

Wiggins made a large circle around the hole, then began to pace, the cockiness that he always exuded conspicuously absent. What was wrong? Did he sense his days of freedom were coming to an end?

A half hour later, almost to the minute, another vehicle came up the drive. This one was much larger, sending a deep vibration through the ground beneath their feet. A large dump truck moved toward the backhoe and the two men standing there. It made a sharp right, then began to back toward the hole. There were no identifying markings, no company logo painted on its doors.

Leaving the truck running, the driver exited and walked the length of it to release a lever on its back. After he returned to the cab, the front of the dump bed began to rise, adding the hiss and whine of hydraulic pistons to the low rumble of the engine. The dump gate, hinged at the top, swung open and a dozen or so fifty-five-gallon drums rolled into the hole.

She cast a glance at Conner. He was still recording, capturing every detail. They had discovered at least one of Wiggins's criminal activities. He was having toxic waste dumped at the mine. They had proof. Tomorrow they would turn the recording over to the police.

Excitement coursed through her, and the black cloud of worry that had hung over her for the past five weeks vanished, giving her a sense of weightlessness. It was almost over. In less than twenty-four hours, she could return home. Her parents and Jayden would be on their way back to Florida. And she would have her life back.

"Hey!"

The sharp word shattered that newfound serenity and sent shards of panic spiking through her. She shifted her gaze back to the men. All activity had ceased. Wiggins stood with his arm outstretched, index finger pointed in their direction. The backhoe operator stood next to him, eyes scouring the woods. The door to the dump truck swung open, and the driver dropped to the ground. He, too, joined the others.

Darci swayed as terror crashed down on her. They had been discovered.

Conner lowered the camera, panic scattering his thoughts. They were outnumbered three to two. And more than likely, at least one of the men was armed. People who did their business under cover of darkness usually were.

Without taking his eyes from Wiggins and his cronies, he reached for Darci's hand. If they ran, the men would hear them and be on them in moments. But if they stayed where they were, they would be sitting ducks. The record light on the camera, as small as it was, had given away their position. He needed to call 911.

But there was no time. Wiggins moved toward them, the other men flanking him.

"Turn over the camera, Tucker, and no one will get hurt."

Conner squeezed her hand. Wiggins was a liar. As soon as he had the evidence in his possession, he would kill them both.

He stuffed the camera into his jacket pocket. "Run!" His command was a sharp hiss.

Darci didn't hesitate. She jerked her hand from his and sprinted away, her path carrying her deeper into the woods. He stayed right on her heels. Heavy footsteps sounded behind them.

Wiggins's girth would hold him back. They could easily outrun him. But the truck driver looked to be in excellent shape. The backhoe operator was huge, like a grizzly. But grizzlies were deceptively fast.

A shot rang out, and pine bark peppered his right cheek and arm like shrapnel. That was too close. They had a chance of outrunning the men, but not their bullets.

Then Darci stumbled in front of him and went down with a thud and a grunt. He couldn't stop, couldn't change direction, couldn't even take a panicked leap over her. One foot caught her body, and for a half moment, he went airborne. Then he, too, hit the ground. Nicki's too-large shoes. He should have brought her some that fit.

The footsteps grew louder. He held up a hand, motioning her to stay still. They couldn't run now. The men were too close.

"Stop." The command came from either the truck driver or the backhoe operator.

The forest fell silent, except for some rustling in the distance, probably Wiggins bringing up the rear.

"Listen." It was the same voice as before.

"I don't hear anything."

"That's my point, you idiot. They've stopped running."

Conner tried to still his breathing and sent up a silent prayer. Darci was likely doing the same. As long as the men didn't pass too close, the underbrush would help conceal them, even though it wasn't as thick as in the summertime.

A flashlight beam swept the area, passing right over their heads, and Conner flattened himself against the ground.

"Get your tails in gear." Wiggins had almost caught up to the others and wasn't happy to see them idle. His tread was heavy, and he wheezed as he walked.

The same man who had called for the halt answered. "They're close by. We'd probably hear them if we didn't have Sasquatch lumbering through the forest with us."

Wiggins countered the insult with a threat. "If you let them get away, you're going to wish all you had to deal with was Sasquatch."

He now stood with the other men, all of them only twenty feet away. The glow of a cell phone illuminated Wiggins's face, then disappeared as he pressed it to his ear. Conner's own phone was still in his pocket, if he hadn't broken it during his fall. As desperate as he was to make that 911 call, he didn't dare try.

Finally Wiggins spoke. "You'd better get out here. Your girlfriend just videotaped everything."

Conner didn't miss Wiggins's sneer on the word *girlfriend*. Who was he talking to, Fuller?

Wiggins spoke again, this time louder. "I'm giving you one more chance to give yourself up, Tucker. Give me the camera, and I'll let you walk out of here."

Conner waited. Darci wouldn't fall for it. She was too smart.

"Fine. Have it your way." The cell phone

came out again. Several seconds passed in silence before Wiggins spoke again. "Go get him. We need some insurance."

Go get who? An answer tried to weave its way into his mind, but he shut it out. Jayden was with Darci's parents. They would have arrived in North Carolina hours ago.

Unless they never made it out of Levy County. Or maybe Wiggins's men followed them to Murphy, just in case they needed to pull that card. A sick sense of dread settled over him. If anything happened to Jayden, it would kill Darci.

If Wiggins didn't kill her first. He sent up another prayer.

"Listen up." Wiggins was in commander mode. "You two spread out, keep looking. I'm getting the dog."

Conner's breath hitched as a new fear gripped him. Wiggins was coming back with Genghis. Although the pit knew him, he didn't know Darci. But if commanded to attack, it wouldn't matter whether the dog knew him or not.

The two men moved away, deeper into the woods, as Wiggins backtracked. Over the next several minutes, the crunch of dried leaves sounded all around them, gradually fading. The men were combing the forest for them.

Conner raised himself to a crouch and pulled out his cell phone. He couldn't call 911 without being overheard. But he could send Hunter a text and pray with everything in him that the officer had his phone on him. Concealing the light as well as he could with his jacket, he keyed in the message—At mine. SOS. Send help. He would attempt the 911 call later.

He rose without making a sound, then helped Darci to her feet. Since the men had moved farther ahead, their best bet would be to go back the way Wiggins had, then head for the road. If they could make it to his bike, they could escape.

They retraced their steps, moving more slowly than they had earlier, more concerned with stealth than speed. Actually, they needed to be concerned with both. Soon Wiggins would be back with Genghis. *God, please let us reach the bike first.*

A deep, menacing bark pierced the still night, putting some speed in his step. The barking grew closer, then became frenzied. Genghis had smelled them, or maybe heard them. He was hot on their trail.

Conner stepped over a downed tree and bent to tuck the camera into a fork. If they escaped, he would bring the authorities back with him to retrieve it. If Wiggins caught them, he would use it as a bargaining chip.

Stealth forgotten, he grabbed Darci's hand and bounded through the woods, pulling her along. A minute later, the trees disappeared, and they skidded to a stop at the edge of the road.

Conner looked both directions.

His heart fell.

They had missed his bike by a good quarter mile.

Darci's heart pounded and her breath came in gasps. Her ribs still hurt from the beating Wiggins's men had given her last night.

But she'd pushed her body to the maximum of what it could endure. All for nothing. They'd reached the road, the bike was nowhere to be seen and the dog would be on them within moments.

Headlights moved toward them, and hope sparked inside her. Maybe they could flag down the driver and be gone before Wiggins and the dog emerged from the woods.

But Wiggins had called Fuller. And he'd told him to get out there. What if it was Fuller behind the wheel?

The vehicle sped toward them, then screeched

to a stop. It was a silver SUV. The driver's window lowered. Doug sat at the wheel.

Relief washed through her, so intense her knees almost buckled. "We need your help. I don't have time to explain, but—"

Her own gasp cut off her words as realization slammed into her. "No."

She shook her head and took a step backward, pulling Conner with her.

The man with the raspy voice. It wasn't Fuller. It was Doug. The call Wiggins had made was to Doug.

She spun around in time to see a huge pit bull emerge from the woods, straining at its leash. Fangs glistened in the moonlight.

Wiggins appeared a moment later. "Heel."

The dog lunged toward them, almost pulling Wiggins with it. Low growls rumbled in its throat, punctuated by vicious barks. The dog's chest was massive, its jaws powerful. If Wiggins let go of that leash, she and Conner would be torn to shreds.

Wiggins gave the command again and the dog stood down. With the beast now under control, Wiggins put the leash around one wrist and pulled out his phone. The run had left him gasping for air, but he managed two short sentences. "Come back in. I've got 'em."

When she cast a glance over her shoulder,

Doug was still inside the vehicle, his mouth set in a grim line. Was it coldness she saw on his face? Determination?

Or was there a battle going on behind those dark eyes, a decision to make, whether to side with her or with Wiggins?

No, she was grasping at straws. When offered a choice between doing for someone else and taking care of number one, Doug's course of action was always the same. He would never give up his wealth or his freedom, even in exchange for her life.

"Get in, both of you." Wiggins's words cut across her thoughts. He had pocketed the phone and stood ten feet away, with a pistol aimed at them.

Darci complied and started to slide across the seat to make room for Conner. Pain pierced her right side, and she gasped.

Doug studied her in the soft glow of the dome light. His eyes narrowed. "What happened to you?"

"Ask Wiggins." She pressed her hands into the seat to move toward the center and winced.

Anger flared in Doug's eyes, and he charged from the truck. "What did you do?"

Wiggins snorted. "What you wouldn't."

Darci's gaze bounced between her ex and her boss. Doug was self-centered and egotistical, but she'd never known him to be a crook. So how did he get mixed up with someone like Wiggins?

Conner's hand slid behind him and re-emerged with his phone. Hope surged through her. If he could call 911 while Wiggins and Doug were outside the vehicle, they might have a chance. He'd already texted someone. But she'd been too busy running for her life to ask him about it.

Keeping the phone between them, he swiped the screen to unlock it. But that was as far as he got.

"Come on." Wiggins angled his head toward the vehicle. "Let's get these two back to the mine."

Conner slipped the phone under his leg. Her own was of no use to them. When they fled, she'd left her purse lying on the blanket, both phones inside.

Doug sighed and stepped into the driver's door opening. "All right. Get in."

Wiggins headed toward the back of the vehicle, and Doug turned in the seat. His gaze locked with Conner's and narrowed. Darci tensed. The chances of Doug helping her, however slim, would probably be better if Conner wasn't with her.

The door behind them opened, and the dog

heaved itself in. Within seconds, hot breath brushed the back of her head and panting filled her ears. The dog was no threat now. It had been commanded to stand down. But having those razor-sharp teeth so close to her neck kept her on edge.

The door slammed shut, and Wiggins made his way along the passenger's side. Conner would have no opportunity to call 911 now. And they wouldn't get help from anyone else. Not a single car had passed.

Wiggins heaved his bulk into the seat and turned, training his weapon on them. "Don't even think of trying anything."

When they pulled into the drive leading to the mine, headlights were moving toward them. Someone was leaving. She watched the vehicle draw closer. Its headlights were too high and widely spaced to belong to the pickup. It was the dump truck. Apparently the driver didn't have the stomach for whatever was going to happen next. Or didn't want to be a witness.

She stared at the back of Doug's head. He was the father of her child. There had been strong feelings between them at one point. Maybe he still felt something for her. But in the end, it wouldn't matter.

Doug drew to a stop near the backhoe, and Wiggins stepped from the vehicle.

"Get out."

Conner slipped his phone into his front pocket and slid from the Escalade. After helping her to the ground, his eyes locked with hers. This gentle, caring man had done everything in his power to keep her safe, and she loved him for it.

He leaned forward to brush a kiss on her cheek, letting his mouth linger close to her ear.

"I texted Hunter." His words came out in the softest whisper.

And they endeared him to her even more. Their situation was as bleak as it could be. But he wanted to give her hope.

"Stand over there." Wiggins made a sideways swipe with the gun. Doug had gotten out of the truck, too, but Genghis was still inside.

Conner took her hand, and they moved away from the hole. The backhoe operator had just about finished filling it in. In a few more minutes, he would be ready to level it out, leaving behind no evidence of what had gone on over the past hour.

Wiggins pointed the gun at her head. "Hand over the camera."

"I don't have it."

He released a sigh and shook his head, as if

he was dealing with a troublesome child. "It looks like we're going to have to do this my way."

Still holding the gun, he once again pulled out his phone. After a swipe and a couple of touches, he put it to his ear.

"Darci here needs a little motivation." A devious smile curled his lips. "Oh, yeah. That's good."

He touched the screen again and turned the phone toward her. At first she didn't hear anything. Then there was soft whimpering.

Dear God, no. Please don't let it be Jayden.

The whimpering faded, and a female voice came through the phone, weak and quivery. "Hello? Sweetheart?"

Recognition slammed into her, dropping her to her knees. Her chest constricted, and the steel bands worked their way higher, her throat tightening until she could no longer breathe.

She knew that voice. And she knew those whimpers.

Wiggins's men had found her parents and Jayden in North Carolina.

TWELVE

Darci squeezed her eyes shut against the tears welling up and pressed her hands over her face. The next moment, Conner was on his knees beside her, gathering her into his arms.

"Leave her parents and that little boy alone. They have nothing to do with any of this." Anger emanated from him. His voice shook with it.

Darci lowered her hands and looked up at Doug. He stood to the side, jaw tight, dark eyes unreadable. He might not care what happened to her parents, but Jayden was his own flesh and blood. He had to at least feel something for him.

Wiggins crossed his arms. "Everything depends on you two. I'm willing to make a trade. The camera for the lives of your parents and son."

Conner stood, pulling her to her feet with

him. Wiggins had said nothing about *their* lives. Those were already forfeit.

"The camera's mine." The strength in Conner's tone was reassuring. "I hid it in the woods. But I can take you there."

Wiggins paused for a moment, raking them both with that cool gaze. "Never mind. We'll find it ourselves. And if we don't, after a few good rains, it won't matter anyway."

He signaled the backhoe operator. "We'll put them next to the girl."

The girl. Claire. The words were like a kick to the gut. Deep down, she'd known Claire hadn't just taken off. But hearing Wiggins's words had slammed the door shut on that slim chance that she was still out there somewhere, in hiding, but alive.

The words had affected Conner the same way they had her. Grief had settled into the lines of his face, now pasty white in the moonlight.

The backhoe operator moved his equipment farther back and closer to the woods. Then he raised the bucket and began to dig. Darci's eyes returned to Doug. His jaw was still tight, but he was no longer standing still. He shifted his weight from one foot to the other and clenched and unclenched his fists. He was a pressure cooker, slowly building to an explosion.

"I'm not going to stand by and watch you kill them." His words were surprisingly controlled.

Hope surged through her. Maybe Doug *did* care for her enough to defy Wiggins.

Wiggins raised his brows and nailed him with that condescending gaze that he'd perfected so well. "You don't have to watch. Cover your eyes if you can't handle it. If you'd kept her close like you were told, we wouldn't be having this conversation."

Conner squeezed her hand and took a small step backward. Within seconds she followed his move, realizing his intent. The backhoe operator was occupied. And Doug had distracted Wiggins. The woods were just thirty feet behind them. The move was bold and reeked of desperation, but it might be the only chance they had of saving themselves.

"Hey, I tried." Doug's tone was defensive. "She wouldn't have anything to do with me."

Darci's eyes widened, that hope disappearing as suddenly as it had come. Doug didn't care for her. It was all a farce. He'd renewed contact with her only because Wiggins had told him to.

"Apparently you didn't try hard enough."

"I did. I threatened to fight for custody of the kid. I even tried to *scare* her into my arms."

Scare her? What was he talking about?

The intruder outside her window. The pipe bomb. Both incidents had happened when Doug was there to play the hero. It wasn't coincidence. He'd set them up. But what about the car that ran her off the road?

She took another small step back, her hand still in Conner's. They had covered about five of the thirty feet, and Wiggins and Doug were still embroiled in their argument.

Wiggins continued, "When you set out to scare someone, you've got to do it right, not mess with stupid kid stuff."

Doug's fists tightened again. "Like slamming into them? You could have seriously hurt her or the boy."

The boy. He had yet to call Jayden by his name. Because there was no bond. Regardless of how things turned out tonight, Doug wouldn't be the one raising her son. The realization brought a level of comfort.

The backhoe operator stopped digging and turned off the machine. "Let's get it done. I don't want to be here all night."

A high-pitched whine sounded in the distance, so faint at first she was afraid she'd imagined it. But the panic that flashed across Doug's face told her she hadn't. The backhoe operator heard the sirens, too. He jumped down from his perch and ran full speed toward his pickup.

Conner's text to Hunter. It had gotten through. Conner had never been able to call 911, but Hunter had.

The sirens grew louder, and Wiggins raised the gun.

No. Help was so close. They only needed to hold out for a few more minutes.

"Wiggins, don't do this. It's over. The police are on the way. Don't add murder to your crimes."

"I already have. And I'm not leaving witnesses."

She shifted her gaze to Doug, who stood just six feet from Wiggins. But he didn't meet her eyes. He stood ramrod straight, his hands curled into tight fists, tension radiating from him. If she could get him to look at her, to recall what he'd felt for her during their college days...

"Doug, please—"

Wiggins cocked the gun and aimed it at her. She cast a desperate glance at Conner. They were still a good twenty feet from the woods, too far to make a run for it.

A shot rang out. At the same moment, Conner slammed into her, knocking her sideways. She managed to regain her footing. Conner didn't. He dropped to his knees, hands clutching his right side.

"No!" She knelt beside him and wrapped him in her arms. He'd bought her a few extra seconds but sacrificed himself.

Wiggins raised the gun again, and she braced herself for the searing pain. But it didn't come. Before Wiggins could pull the trigger, Doug took a flying leap and tackled him, bringing him to the ground. The weapon discharged, and for several tense moments, they fought over it, until Doug was able to wrest it free.

"Are you crazy?" Wiggins let out an angry bellow, then threw a punch, connecting with the younger man's jaw.

"No, I'm saner than I've ever been in my life. And I won't be a partner to your crimes any longer."

The sirens were closer now, loud and shrill as the vehicles moved up the drive. Conner slumped against her, and she gently lowered him to the ground until he was resting on his back. The side of his jacket fell away, revealing a huge dark stain spreading across his shirt. His chest rose and fell in shallow pants, and his eyes drifted closed.

She pressed her hands against his side, trying to stem the flow of blood. "Hang on, Conner. Don't you dare leave me. I love you."

His eyes fluttered open, and he tried to lift a hand to her face. Halfway there, he dropped it, and his eyes closed again. She struggled to stifle a sob, but it escaped anyway.

The sirens grew to ear-piercing levels, setting her teeth on edge and shredding her nerves. Red and blue flashed all around her. Then there was silence, broken only by Wiggins's angry voice. He was still castigating Doug.

Strong hands gripped her shoulders and she jerked her head around. A Levy County deputy leaned over her.

"Let us tend to him."

She allowed him to help her to her feet and wiped her hands on her pants. Two paramedics were hurrying toward them carrying a stretcher and their tactical responder cases. *Yes.* Hunter hadn't just called for law enforcement. He'd requested an ambulance, just in case. It could very well save Conner's life.

"My parents and son." She grasped the deputy's arm, panic in her tone.

"Where are they?"

"At their place in North Carolina." She gave him the address. "They're being held hostage."

The deputy spoke into his radio, and Wiggins's voice erupted again, pulling her gaze that direction.

"You think you're going to have it any easier in jail?" He jabbed an index finger at Doug. "Because that's where you're gonna be, boy. All those burly tough guys are going to have fun with you."

A Levy County Sheriff's deputy clicked cuffs around Wiggins's wrists. But it didn't stop the flow of hateful words spilling from his mouth.

"You'll never make it. You're weak. I've been telling you that since you were seven years old."

What? Wiggins had known Doug as a child? How?

The deputy gripped Wiggins's arm and led him toward the patrol car. He was trying to give him his rights, but Wiggins wasn't shutting up for anyone.

"In almost twenty-five years, I should have been able to make a man out of you. But that wimp of a father of yours didn't leave me anything to work with."

Darci's jaw dropped as it suddenly clicked. The link between Wiggins and Doug. Wiggins was the stepfather that Doug had hated for most of his life.

The two paramedics jogged past her carrying Conner on the stretcher. As they loaded him into the ambulance, she pressed a fist to her mouth and fought back tears. *Lord, please let him be okay.*

The doors slammed shut, and a deputy approached her. She had plenty to tell him, starting with the overheard conversation in her office. Maybe the activity would help keep her sane while Conner was rushed to the hospital.

She began her story, glancing to her right as Wiggins was put into one of the police cars. His face was still contorted in anger.

Doug's wasn't. As a deputy led him past her toward a second vehicle, his eyes locked with hers. She mouthed the words *thank you*, and one side of his mouth lifted, the hint of a smile. An odd sort of contentment seemed to have settled over him. He'd sacrificed his own freedom to save her life. Maybe he *did* still care for her. Or maybe he'd just jumped on the only chance he saw to be free of his stepfather's control.

Maybe he could get a lighter sentence for cooperating and testifying against his stepdad. She hoped so. Before she finished her statement, she would tell the deputy about Doug tackling Wiggins. If he hadn't acted when he had, things would have turned out quite differently.

Two more vehicles made their way up the drive, Hunter's Tundra and another Levy

County Sheriff's. A deputy got out of the car and approached her. "Right before getting to the mine, we saw someone pulling out of the drive. We need to see if you can identify him."

She raised her brows. "Big guy in a light-colored Ford Ranger pickup? Blue jeans and flannel shirt?"

"Yeah."

The deputy led her to his vehicle. The man she described was inside, head lowered. When the deputy opened the door, the man looked up. His eyes were a vivid blue.

She nodded. "He's the backhoe operator and one of Wiggins's goons." She motioned toward her face. "What you see here is courtesy of his fists."

"Looks like we'll be adding battery to whatever other charges we come up with."

She glanced at the truck sitting behind the deputy's vehicle. Hunter was moving toward her. For many years, he'd been a good friend. Tonight he'd saved her life. Then Conner had saved it again by pushing her out of the way and taking her bullet. Doug had saved it a third time.

Another deputy hurried toward her. "We just got a call from Cherokee County. Your parents and son are safe."

Darci's breath whooshed out in a relieved

sigh, along with all her strength. If Hunter hadn't steadied her, she might have fallen.

Thank You, Lord.

In spite of everything she'd been through, she had a lot to be thankful for. Wiggins was in custody. She was safe. Her parents and Jayden were safe.

There was only one more prayer to be answered. And she would plead with everything in her for a positive outcome.

Dear God, please let Conner pull through.

Darci raised both arms and leaned over the back of her chair, enjoying the satisfying crack of her spine loosening. An older issue of one of the popular women's magazines lay open in her lap. At the moment, she couldn't remember which one. That was how thoroughly it had engaged her.

But it wasn't the fault of the magazine. Except for those occasions when she'd gotten up to pace the waiting room floor, she'd sat in the same chair all night, alternating between worrying over Conner and praying for him. A few times she'd dozed, then woken up with her head cocked painfully sideways and her neck in spasm.

Two hours ago, she'd gotten the news she'd been waiting for. Conner was out of surgery.

The bullet had been removed and the damage to the large and small intestines repaired. No vital organs had been hit. His chances of surviving were high.

She turned the page, and her eyes fell on yet another article that she didn't really see. Conner had finally woken up thirty minutes ago and been transferred to a room. She would be able to go in and see him shortly, as soon as his mother and stepfather left.

The first thing she'd done on arriving at the hospital was to ask for his phone so she could call his family. And when the doctor had said he was awake and could have visitors, she'd insisted that they go in first. They were family. She was... Now that everything was over, she wasn't sure what she was to him. And she wasn't ready to learn. For now, it was enough to know that he had made it through his surgery and was going to be okay.

A short time later, his parents came back to thank her and tell her goodbye. She made her way toward Conner's room, and when she stepped inside, her heart lurched. He lay on his back with his eyes closed. Unshed tears stung her eyes, and she had to swallow past a sudden lump in her throat. He looked so pale against the white sheets, his strength sapped.

She approached the bed and his eyes opened.

The smile he gave her was weak, but it still made her stomach flip.

She smiled back. "How are you feeling?"

"I've had better days." The words came out slurred. He was likely on some pretty heavy-duty painkillers. "But I'm alive." His eyes closed in a prolonged blink, reopening several seconds later. "A few hours ago, I didn't think I'd be able to say that."

She sat in the chair next to the bed, and he reached over to squeeze her hand. "Thanks for calling Mom."

He released her to pick up a cup from the rolling table. When he tipped it, ice rattled. He shook several of the chips into his mouth and let them melt. "If they don't bring me some water soon, I might have you fill this at the sink."

"Not me. If you're going to try to circumvent the doctor's orders, you'll have to find a different accomplice."

"You're no fun." The grin he gave her was lopsided, as if it required too much effort to lift both sides of his mouth.

He let his eyes drift closed again, then started to speak without opening them.

"It looks like my fatherhood days are over."

"What do you mean?"

He opened his eyes. "Mom and Tony are picking up Kyle."

Sadness bore down on her, an unexplainable sense of loss. Parenthood was a common thread between them, that invisible bond that connected his life to hers.

She forced a smile. "So your stepdad has finally decided he's recovered?"

"Or he feels my bullet wound is more serious than his six-month-old heart attack."

"So you're free. What are you going to do now?"

"Turn in my two-week notice. I won't leave them in a lurch." His mouth cocked up again. "They're already short one CFO." He shifted his position, then winced. "How about you?"

"I don't know. With Wiggins out of the picture, I could probably get my old job back." But for some reason, she didn't feel ready. What she really needed was a time of healing, surrounded by the peace and tranquility of Cedar Key and the love of friends and family.

Conner's eyes drifted closed again. This time they didn't reopen until she spoke.

"I'm going to let you get some rest."

"I'm sorry. I'm not very good company."

"You have an excuse."

He reached for her hand. "You'll come back?" His eyes closed. "No, it's too far."

"I'll be back tomorrow. I promise."

Moments later, his grip relaxed, and she slid her hand from his. Yes, she would be back, because she loved him. Her heart twisted, the longing inside almost breaking it in two.

Conner's fatherhood days were over. But she would always be a mother. So they would never be more than friends.

She picked up her pace, suddenly anxious to be home. Not her house in Gulf Hammock. *Home*. Cedar Key.

When she got to her car, her phone rang. It was Hunter. He had given her a ride from the mine to her house in Gulf Hammock, and she had texted him updates on Conner throughout the night. Now it was his turn.

"They're making headway on the case."

"Already?"

"Doug is being super cooperative, spilling everything. He hasn't just thrown Wiggins under the bus. He's backed it up and run over him."

She smiled. "There's a lot of bad blood between them. Wiggins is Doug's stepfather."

"Interesting. Did Wiggins know who you were when they hired you?"

"I don't know." The first interview she'd had was with Turlong. The second was with Wiggins. Even though Turlong had the final say, he would have listened to Wiggins's input.

"How's Conner?"

"Pretty doped up, but good. I'm leaving the hospital now."

"I'll keep you posted on what I find out. The way it looks, Wiggins was involved in a lot more than just dumping toxic waste."

After ending the call with Hunter, she stopped for breakfast, then began the hour-and-fifteen-minute drive to Cedar Key. It gave her time to think. For the first time ever, she had no direction for her life.

She'd given up the store to work at the mine. But the thought of going back there left her cold. She'd have to make a decision soon. She wasn't in a financial position to spend weeks making up her mind.

When she reached Cedar Key, she didn't turn right to go to her parents' house. They had left North Carolina at first light but wouldn't be home for several more hours. And she had no desire to sit alone in an empty house.

Instead, she continued down D Street to Second, then eased to a stop in front of the store. Meagan had it all decked out for Christmas. Light-filled garlands framed the front window, and glittered stars and snowflakes hung at varying levels behind the glass.

As Darci reached for the doorknob, a sense of nostalgia crept over her, maybe even a little bit of homesickness, which didn't make sense since she came home every weekend. But she missed being a part of everyday life in Cedar Key. And she missed her store.

She swung open the door and stepped inside. Meagan's artistic touch was visible there also. Christmas lights and garlands were draped throughout, and one of the displays had been moved to make room for a tree. It wasn't decorated with a hodgepodge of ornaments and tinsel tossed on without care. It was a work of art, with flowers, ribbons, snowflakes and a variety of glass shapes, everything in silver and white.

Meagan rushed forward and wrapped her in a gentle hug. "I've been so worried about you. Hunter's been keeping us posted."

"Thanks. It's good to finally be home. I actually get to sleep in my own bed tonight." Her Cedar Key one, anyway. Her bedroom at her parents' house had remained essentially unchanged since she was fifteen.

"So what are you going to do now?"

It was the same question Conner had asked. And she still didn't have an answer. "Wiggins fired me, but I don't know if he hired anyone to replace me yet. Since he's not there anymore,

I suppose I could walk in as if nothing happened and see if they throw me out."

Meagan seemed to be assessing her. "You don't look very excited about that prospect."

Darci sighed. "No, I guess not. Frankly, after everything I've been through the past few weeks, I just want to come home."

"I can understand that."

Darci's gaze shifted to one of the paintings that Meagan had displayed. "I like this one." It was a scene of a beach with a piece of driftwood. In the background, waves rose in a random series of peaks, curls and sea spray. "It has a more mystical, fairy-tale feel to it than your other paintings."

"I've been experimenting with some different styles and techniques."

Even though Darci was studying the painting, she could feel Meagan's eyes on her.

Meagan continued, "Everything has been selling almost as quickly as I can get it finished, and I'm doing quite a few commissioned paintings. I'm having a hard time keeping up with it all."

Darci met her friend's gaze. Meagan wasn't just chatting. She had something on her mind.

"I'm close to the point that I could almost make a full-time income from my painting, especially if I promoted myself, worked with a few galleries."

Darci's heart started to race. Was Meagan saying what she thought she was?

"I never changed the name of the store. It's still Darci's Collectibles and Gifts." She leaned back against the counter. "If you wanted to buy it back, you wouldn't even have to replace the sign."

"Are you serious?"

"Totally. If you don't want it, don't worry. I'll still keep making the payments. But if you want to come back, we can work something out."

The cloud of uncertainty dissipated, and a sense of contentment swept through her. She could make it. She'd been making it before. It had just been tight, especially with having to pay for her and Jayden's insurance coverage. But she'd done it before and she could do it again. First she would pray about it and ask for guidance.

She'd prayed before taking the job at P. T. also. But had she prayed earnestly, or had she already had her mind made up?

It was a question she couldn't answer without a lot of soul-searching. Right decision or not, some good had come from it. If she'd never taken the job, she would never have met

Conner. And chances were good that he would never have found justice for Claire.

Now that it was over, what would become of her and Conner? They often shared meals and let the boys play together. And they'd made it a habit to go to church together on Sundays, the four of them. But Kyle was no longer living with Conner. Would she and Jayden ever see him again?

Without Kyle or the investigation, would Conner have any reason to see her? The thought left her with a hollow emptiness inside.

She would likely end up taking over the store and moving back to Cedar Key on a full-time basis. The decision just felt right. Sometime soon, her work life would be settled.

Unfortunately, her personal life was nowhere close.

THIRTEEN

Conner rinsed his breakfast dishes and put them in the dishwasher. Bacon and eggs. That was his specialty. But he'd hardly tasted them. Now they sat like lead in his gut.

Claire was gone. He'd suspected it since the moment she disappeared. But he'd always held out some sliver of hope that she'd simply gone into hiding to save her life. Thursday night, though, while he was on his way to the hospital, they'd recovered her body. And that made it final.

And Kyle was gone, too. Conner's parents had taken him back. So now he was free, responsible for no one but himself. This was what he'd looked forward to for the past six months.

So why did he feel as if he'd lost everything dear to him?

He strode toward the living room, trying to tamp down the antsiness poking at him. He needed to move, to do something strenuous to work out his frustration. Yard work was out of the question. So was lifting weights or pounding out his dissatisfaction on the tennis court. Darci had brought him home from the hospital yesterday, with strict instructions in hand. He was to do basically nothing.

When he reached the living room, hundreds of tiny lights shone from in front of the window. He'd flipped the switch out of habit when he passed through on his way to fix breakfast.

It was Christmas Eve. But the beautifully decorated tree didn't cheer him. In fact, it mocked him. For a brief moment, he'd held something wonderful in his hands. But before he could tighten his grip and capture it, it had slipped through his fingers.

The day they bought and set up the tree, Kyle's excited chatter and Darci's sweet voice had filled the house. And for the first time in many years, he'd looked forward to the holiday with a childlike excitement. He'd gotten a small taste of what it meant to be part of a real family, and it had left him with a longing for more—a longing that would likely never be satisfied.

He sank down on the couch and stared at the tree. Kyle had been the one to attach the hooks to every one of the ornaments. And he'd hung a good one third of them. The placement wasn't always the best, but Kyle was proud of what he'd done, and Conner wouldn't dream of moving a single piece.

The way he was missing the kid had caught him totally off guard. He missed the knowledge that he was living for someone other than himself, and he missed having another living person in the house. He even missed the complaining.

With Kyle, there had been constant activity—running through the house to ask what was for dinner or if they could go somewhere, battles over homework and explosions and zings of lasers once said homework had been completed. Today, instead of surrounding him with warmth and vitality, the cold, still house wrapped him in silence.

But he wouldn't wish Kyle back, no matter how much the loneliness dogged him. Kyle was better off being raised by his grandparents. After over thirty years of failure, his mother was finally in a position to provide a stable home. And Tony seemed like a good man. The two of them had been together for four years.

He pushed himself to his feet. Kyle was no longer living with him, but that didn't have to stop him from still being a part of the kid's life.

He started to retrieve his keys from the hook

by the door, but his hand stopped in midair. That was another one of his restrictions—no driving. If he showed up at his mother's house in his truck, she would wring his neck.

When he called her to ask for a ride, she was thrilled.

"Kyle's been mopey ever since we brought him home."

Conner smiled. "That's pretty much par for the course." Kyle had displayed plenty of that mopeyness at his place, too.

"I think he misses you."

"It seems strange to admit it, but I miss him, too."

Ten minutes later, Tony pulled up in his driveway and Conner slid into the front seat of the Cadillac. Today he would hang out at his mom's place. Or maybe he would see if they could all take Kyle somewhere.

Cedar Key.

No. He couldn't keep seeking out Darci. She'd fallen in love with him. She had told him the night he was shot. Of course, at the time she said it, she was afraid he was going to die.

But that didn't lessen the meaning of the words or diminish the importance of what she felt for him. It was in her eyes every time she looked at him.

And that was why he needed to tell her

goodbye. Darci deserved someone who would be a good father and a good husband. He would be neither. And delaying the inevitable would only make it harder for everyone.

When he walked into his mother's house, Kyle was sitting on the living room couch, a game controller in his hands. He cast a quick sideways glance Conner's direction, then did a double take.

The controller hit the floor with a thud. The next moment, Kyle was on his feet, running full speed toward the door. At the last minute, Conner turned to offer his good side. Then Kyle hit him with such force, he had to take a couple of steps backward to regain his balance.

"Whoa, buddy." He laughed. "If I didn't know better, I'd think you were happy to see me."

"I want to go home."

"This *is* your home now. Grandma and Grandpa are going to take care of you."

Kyle squeezed him even more tightly. "But I don't want to stay here. I want to live with you and Darci and Jayden."

He disentangled himself from Kyle's grasp and dropped to one knee in front of him, putting them almost eye to eye. "Darci and Jayden don't live with me."

"Where are they?"

"Cedar Key."

"Well, go get them."

Conner sighed. Kyle made it sound so easy. And in his seven-year-old mind, it was. Kids could never see how complicated life really was.

And adults often made it more complicated than it needed to be.

He stood, and an image planted itself in his mind—he and Darci and the two boys, a family. Lead filled his gut. Could he do it? Could he learn how to be a good husband and father?

Not unless he completely let go of the past. With God's help, maybe he could do it.

God, I'm not giving you much to work with, but this is all I've got. Make me into the kind of man you want me to be.

Beneath the fear and uncertainty, a seed of hope sprouted. He didn't have to follow in the footsteps of his father.

He took Kyle's hand and turned toward his mom. "How would you guys like to be tourists for a day?"

If they couldn't do it, he would call a friend. Or a cab. He would walk if he had to. One way or another, he was going to see Darci.

Maybe he didn't have to be perfect. Maybe love and a good dose of humility would cover a lot of mistakes, both as a mate and as a parent.

* * *

A cold breeze blew through the park, and Darci drew her coat more tightly around her. Yesterday's rain had ushered in a cold front, making it feel more like Christmas.

In the daylight, the park didn't appear much different from any other time of the year. But once the sun set, it would be transformed into a sparkling fairyland of lights, with dozens of strands draped over bushes and in trees. More had been spiraled around lampposts, and the pavilion boasted several lit wreaths. Around town, lighted shapes graced the poles that lined the streets, not the usual angels, bells and candles, but everything beach-themed—pelicans, seahorses, shells, starfish and dolphins.

Darci picked up the phone lying in her lap. She'd just spoken with Hunter, who had given her another update. The evidence against Wiggins and his cronies was mounting. She had a lot to tell Conner.

If Conner called.

Over the past few days, he seemed to have cooled toward her, or at least become reserved. It had started with her second hospital visit. The first he'd been too out of it to appear anything but sleepy.

But once the anesthesia had fully worn off, each visit thereafter, all the way through the trip home from the hospital, a tense uneasiness had hovered between them. And she was pretty sure she knew why.

Now that he was no longer responsible for Kyle, he was probably looking forward to living it up and fully enjoying the bachelor lifestyle. A lifestyle that would never include taking care of an autistic child.

Which was okay. That had been her plan all along. Once she'd cleared her name and was safe, she and Conner would part ways. Or maintain a casual friendship.

The latter was going to be more difficult than she'd ever dreamed. Because she'd fallen in love with him. And she'd been stupid enough to tell him. Of course, he had just been shot. He might not even remember. But his uncharacteristic stiffness around her said that he did.

So he was trying to untangle himself from her. He didn't have anything to worry about. She was just as prepared to walk away as he was. Jayden needed her, and she wouldn't give up that responsibility to anyone. It was one she cherished.

She watched him climb the metal rungs, then held her phone in the air and captured the scene with a soft click. The bright yellow and blue of the playground equipment stood out against the gray backdrop of water and sky, a palm tree to the side. On one of the platforms, Jayden stood in profile, watching the other children play. At least that was what he appeared to be doing. She was never really sure.

When she lifted her eyes from the screen, a boy ran onto the playground from the parking lot behind her, and she sat up straighter. With his height and build and hair color, he could be Kyle. She pivoted on the bench, and her heart skipped a beat.

Conner moved toward her, his steps labored, the usual bounce missing. His upper body was cocked slightly to the right, favoring the side where the bullet had entered.

She stood and rounded the bench. "What are you doing here?"

"I came to see you."

"You didn't drive, did you?" She looked around the parking lot, but the blue F-150 wasn't there.

"No, I rode with my mom and stepdad. They decided to do some sightseeing today." He paused and grinned. "At my suggestion."

She motioned toward the bench. "Have a seat. You look like you're in pain."

After settling in next to him, her gaze went back to the playground equipment. Kyle had found Jayden and was talking to him, his posture animated. How much Jayden understood wasn't clear, but he was wearing a soft smile. If she could say that Jayden had actually connected with another child, it would be Kyle.

She brought her attention back to Conner. "I got another update from Hunter. They've made five arrests so far. And I was right. Wiggins was involved in way more than getting rid of toxic waste. From blackmail to bank fraud to forgery, he's had his hands in a little bit of everything."

Her eyes sought out her son, but he was in good hands. Kyle was leading him toward the stairs going up to one of the slides.

"You know that concrete company that listed me as the treasurer? It was basically a shell corporation, doing just enough legal business to appear legitimate. But its primary purpose was to launder the funds that Wiggins received through all his illegal activities. The money would go into the concrete company, backed by fake invoices to contractors, then into the mine's account, backed by more fake invoices for loads of aggregate. Then it would go to United Equipment Corporation for purchases and major repairs of equipment, also backed by fake invoices. I've written checks to them, big checks. It didn't trigger any red flags. Equipment is expensive, both to purchase and to repair."

"So did Wiggins have some involvement with United Equipment?"

"Yeah, vice president. But the big surprise was learning that Doug was the president."

"Interesting. At any rate, it sounds as if Wiggins will be going to jail for a long time. It won't bring Claire back, but I'm glad to see justice being done."

"Me, too. That makes for a pretty cool Christmas present, a little bit of holiday justice." She drew in a deep breath. "You said you came to see me. Was it about anything in particular?" He had something on his mind. Otherwise he would have just called.

He angled himself on the bench so he was facing her a little more fully, his knee resting against hers. "I've enjoyed our time together, and I'm not ready for it to end. I'd like to keep seeing you."

"Seeing me how?"

"Spending time with you because we enjoy each other's company, not because there are bad guys after you."

"Dating?"

"Yes."

She shook her head, her heart twisting in her chest. "I can't. I've got Jayden."

"And I've got Kyle."

She looked at him sharply. "No, you don't. Your parents took him."

"He wants to come back. But he insists that you and Jayden be part of the deal."

"He said that?"

"In so many words."

She sighed and dropped her gaze to her hands folded in her lap. "I still can't. My responsibility is to Jayden. I don't have the time or energy to devote to a relationship."

He took her hands in his. "You don't have to do it alone, Darci. I want to be there for both you and Jayden."

Her defenses began to crack, and she fought to shore them up. "I can't saddle you with that kind of responsibility."

"You're not saddling me with anything. I've already decided to raise Kyle. And he and I have both gotten attached to your little guy."

The admission blew a hole through the wall she had hidden behind for so long. But he continued the barrage.

"You're the one who helped me believe in myself, that I could be a good father and husband in spite of the examples I had growing up. Give me a chance to prove you right."

His words sent the last of the barriers crashing down, leaving her vulnerable and exposed.

For the first time in five years, she was allowing a man access to her heart. The very thought almost sent her into cardiac arrest.

But beneath the fear was anticipation, a sense of excitement over the prospect of a future together.

"Yes." The word was soft and airy. But her heart was beating so wildly in her chest she was having a hard time catching her breath.

Relief flashed across his face, and his eyes grew warm. If she'd doubted what he felt for her before, she didn't any longer.

"I love you, Darci. And I'll do everything in my power to make you happy."

"I love you, too." The words flowed naturally, because this time she knew her love was returned. "I told you I loved you the night you were shot. Did you hear me?"

"Yes, I did. And once I woke up after surgery, I knew I needed to make a decision. I either had to be willing to face my fears and not let my past determine my future, or I needed to sever ties and walk away, without looking back."

"Is that why you've been cool the past few days?"

"Yes. I've been torn."

"So what helped you make your decision?"

A smile spread across his face. "The simple wisdom of a seven-year-old."

She matched his smile with one of her own. "I'll have to remember to thank him."

"I already have."

He leaned toward her, and her eyes fluttered shut. Unlike the last kiss, this one was gentle. Contentment flooded her, the sense that everything was right.

By allowing Conner to share their lives, she wouldn't be taking a piece of herself away from Jayden. Instead she would be bringing more love into his life, that of a big brother and a caring father.

As Conner ended the kiss and backed away, gratitude swelled inside. And she silently thanked God for all His blessings—the mere fact that she was alive, the gift of His Son, the warmth of family and friends and the joy of the season.

She squeezed the hands that held hers and thanked God for one more blessing—the privilege of sharing it all with Conner.

* * * * *

Dear Reader,

Thank you for joining me for another trip back to Cedar Key. I hope you enjoyed Darci and Conner's story.

While writing the first two books, I came to love Darci and her autistic son, Jayden. As someone whose own life has been touched by autism, with the diagnosis in my older grandson, I sympathize with the struggles that parents of autistic children face. Darci had a strong faith, but when everything in her life began to fall apart, she found that faith shaken and had to remind herself that, no matter what happened, God was in control.

Conner was raised in such a dysfunctional family that he felt the only way to avoid the mistakes of his parents was to keep everyone at arm's length. Through his relationship with Darci, he came to understand that with love and a good dose of humility, along with a lot of prayer, he could throw off the chains of his past and be the kind of husband and father he wanted to be.

I hope you'll come back to Cedar Key for Nicki's story and then again when Hunter's sister, Amber, finds her happily-ever-after. In the meantime, I'd love it if you'd drop me a line.

You can find me on Facebook (www.facebook.com/caroljpost.author), Twitter (@caroljpost), my website (www.caroljpost.com) and email (caroljpost@gmail.com). For news and exclusive content, join my newsletter. The link is on my website. I promise I won't sell your info or spam you!

God bless you!
Carol

REQUEST YOUR FREE BOOKS!
2 FREE WHOLESOME ROMANCE NOVELS
IN LARGER PRINT
PLUS 2
FREE
MYSTERY GIFTS

✳✳✳✳✳✳✳✳✳✳✳✳✳✳✳✳✳✳✳✳✳✳

HEARTWARMING™

✳✳✳✳✳✳✳✳✳✳✳✳✳✳✳✳✳✳✳✳✳✳✳✳✳

Wholesome, tender romances

YES! Please send me 2 FREE Harlequin® Heartwarming Larger-Print novels and my 2 FREE mystery gifts (gifts worth about $10). After receiving them, if I don't wish to receive any more books, I can return the shipping statement marked "cancel." If I don't cancel, I will receive 4 brand-new larger-print novels every month and be billed just $5.24 per book in the U.S. or $5.99 per book in Canada. That's a savings of at least 19% off the cover price. It's quite a bargain! Shipping and handling is just 50¢ per book in the U.S. and 75¢ per book in Canada.* I understand that accepting the 2 free books and gifts places me under no obligation to buy anything. I can always return a shipment and cancel at any time. Even if I never buy another book, the two free books and gifts are mine to keep forever.

161/361 IDN GHX2

Name _____

(PLEASE PRINT)

Address _____ Apt. #

City _____ State/Prov. _____ Zip/Postal Code

Signature (if under 18, a parent or guardian must sign)

Mail to the **Reader Service:**
IN U.S.A.: P.O. Box 1867, Buffalo, NY 14240-1867
IN CANADA: P.O. Box 609, Fort Erie, Ontario L2A 5X3

* Terms and prices subject to change without notice. Prices do not include applicable taxes. Sales tax applicable in N.Y. Canadian residents will be charged applicable taxes. Offer not valid in Quebec. This offer is limited to one order per household. Not valid for current subscribers to Harlequin Heartwarming larger-print books. All orders subject to credit approval. Credit or debit balances in a customer's account(s) may be offset by any other outstanding balance owed by or to the customer. Please allow 4 to 6 weeks for delivery. Offer available while quantities last.

Your Privacy—The Reader Service is committed to protecting your privacy. Our Privacy Policy is available online at www.ReaderService.com or upon request from the Reader Service.

We make a portion of our mailing list available to reputable third parties that offer products we believe may interest you. If you prefer that we not exchange your name with third parties, or if you wish to clarify or modify your communication preferences, please visit us at www.ReaderService.com/consumerschoice or write to us at Reader Service Preference Service, P.O. Box 9062, Buffalo, NY 14240-9062. Include your complete name and address.

YES! Please send me **The Montana Mavericks Collection** in Larger Print. This collection begins with 3 FREE books and 2 FREE gifts (gifts valued at approx. $20.00 retail) in the first shipment, along with the other first 4 books from the collection! If I do not cancel, I will receive 8 monthly shipments until I have the entire 51-book Montana Mavericks collection. I will receive 2 or 3 FREE books in each shipment and I will pay just $4.99 US/ $5.89 CDN for each of the other four books in each shipment, plus $2.99 for shipping and handling per shipment.*If I decide to keep the entire collection, I'll have paid for only 32 books, because 19 books are FREE! I understand that accepting the 3 free books and gifts places me under no obligation to buy anything. I can always return a shipment and cancel at any time. My free books and gifts are mine to keep no matter what I decide.

263 HCN 2404   463 HCN 2404

Name	(PLEASE PRINT)	

Address		Apt. #

City	State/Prov.	Zip/Postal Code

Signature (if under 18, a parent or guardian must sign)

Mail to the **Reader Service:**

IN U.S.A.: P.O. Box 1867, Buffalo, NY 14240-1867
IN CANADA: P.O. Box 609, Fort Erie, Ontario L2A 5X3

* Terms and prices subject to change without notice. Prices do not include applicable taxes. Sales tax applicable in N.Y. Canadian residents will be charged applicable taxes. This offer is limited to one order per household. All orders subject to approval. Credit or debit balances in a customer's account(s) may be offset by any other outstanding balance owed by or to the customer. Please allow 4 to 6 weeks for delivery. Offer available while quantities last. Offer not available to Quebec residents.

Your Privacy—The Reader Service is committed to protecting your privacy. Our Privacy Policy is available online at www.ReaderService.com or upon request from the Reader Service.

We make a portion of our mailing list available to reputable third parties that offer products we believe may interest you. If you prefer that we not exchange your name with third parties, or if you wish to clarify or modify your communication preferences, please visit us at www.ReaderService.com/consumerschoice or write to us at Reader Service Preference Service, P.O. Box 9062, Buffalo, NY 14269. Include your complete name and address.

MMLPBPA15

READERSERVICE.COM

Manage your account online!

- Review your order history
- Manage your payments
- Update your address

> *We've designed the*
> *Reader Service website*
> *just for you.*

Enjoy all the features!

- Discover new series available to you, and read excerpts from any series.
- Respond to mailings and special monthly offers.
- Connect with favorite authors at the blog.
- Browse the Bonus Bucks catalog and online-only exculsives.
- Share your feedback.

Visit us at:

ReaderService.com